CONTRACTED FOR THE PETRAKIS HEIR

ANNIE WEST

MILLS & BOON

First Published in Great Britain 2018
by Mills & Boon, an imprint of HarperCollins*Publishers*
1 London Bridge Street, London, SE1 9GF

© 2018 Annie West

ISBN: 978-0-263-93419-9

MIX
Paper from
responsible sources
FSC® C007454

This book is produced from independently certified FSC™ paper
to ensure responsible forest management.
For more information visit www.harpercollins.co.uk/green.

Printed and bound in Spain
by CPI, Barcelona

With smiles and thanks to
Anna C for both prodding and cheering
and Efthalia P for the Greek!

CHAPTER ONE

ADONI PETRAKIS SURVEYED the crowd filling the ballroom of his flagship London hotel. Initially the guests had been on their best behaviour for the wedding ceremony, partly from finding themselves in such a prestigious venue. There had been open-mouthed stares at the soaring antique glass domed ceiling, the recently refurbished hand-blown chandeliers and the other elegant furnishings.

Now the mood bordered on raucous. His school friend Leo's new English in-laws were letting down their hair with abandon.

Adoni's gaze cut to Leo and his bride, now changed out of their church clothes, surrounded by a phalanx of groomsmen playing a drinking game. There was a flurry of bridesmaids in ostentatiously frilled dresses that ranged from pale lemon to a particularly bilious shade of mustard. A braying laugh from one of them scraped like fingernails across a blackboard and Adoni shuddered.

Now the formalities were over, the cake cut, photos taken and speeches delivered, there was nothing keeping him. He'd done his bit, offering Leo the premises for the event and attending in person, even dancing with the bride.

He lifted one shoulder, easing the old stiffness in his collarbone. It had been a long week. A long month for that matter, and while he wasn't ready for bed, nor was he inclined to stay for an increasingly rowdy party. This group had little in common with a man whose life was devoted to business.

If there'd been a woman here he found attractive he might have invited her up to his suite for a private celebration. There wasn't. The only really pretty women were either attached or looked at him with dollar signs in their eyes.

He'd learned his lesson long ago with that breed.

Instead he crossed the room, wished the happy couple all the best, kissed the flushed bride on both cheeks then left. A nod to the hotel events coordinator who was keeping an eye on the evening, then Adoni was in the blessed peace of the atrium.

Since he didn't have company for the night, he'd look over that new contract. Or maybe use the gym.

He was restless, his thoughts on the couple who'd just pledged their lives to each other. And, inevitably, on his own hastily cancelled wedding years ago. His mouth firmed.

He sure as hell didn't carry a torch for Chryssa. Yet it was strange how, all evening, his mind had backtracked to that half-forgotten past, when life had seemed straight-forward and he'd believed in love.

A lifetime ago.

He keyed in the code for his private lift to the owner's suite. The doors slid open and he stepped inside. Seconds later a figure catapulted into the small space, slamming against him in a slither of satin and a cloud of pungent hairspray.

Adoni's nostrils pinched and a sneeze escaped.

'I'm sorry. Did I hurt you?' a husky voice whispered near his chin. 'But please, don't give me away.' Instead of moving back the girl pressed closer, hip to his thigh, hand clawing his sleeve.

'Give you away?'

'Please. He'll hear.' She reached out a pale hand and jabbed the button to make the door close. As soon as it did she released her grip and sank back into the corner.

'Are you okay?' Adoni's voice sharpened. Her head was downcast but the tension in her shoulders and the frenetic pulse at the base of her throat spoke of fear. 'Has some-one hurt you?'

'Hurt me?' She shook her head and straightened away from the wall, swaying a little. 'No, though I'm sure he'd like to strangle me if he could. He hates me and he's a vicious little toad.'

With a gasp she clapped a hand over her mouth and looked up. Unfocused eyes of slate blue met his. Eyes that might have been pretty if it weren't for the huge swathe of too-bright azure eye shadow and the most enormous pair of false eyelashes weighting her lids. She looked like a startled trollop.

'I didn't mean to say that out loud.' She frowned up at him suspiciously as if he'd coaxed the words from her.

'He sounds like a man to avoid.'

'Oh, he is.' The girl nodded so emphatically another acrid wave of hairspray assaulted him. She *was* a girl. Eighteen maybe, twenty max, and trying to look older with that brash make-up. 'If I'd known he was going to be here I'd never have said yes to Emily. Discretion is the better part of valour, after all.'

'Emily?' Adoni crossed his arms and settled his shoulders against the wall, intrigued. Why this unprepossessing female caught his curiosity, he couldn't say. But he was in no hurry. There was nothing waiting in his suite except work and a good brandy.

'The bride.' The frown became a scowl. 'Weren't you at the wedding? I thought I saw you on the other side of the room looking all dark and brooding.' She leaned closer, her gaze intent, and beneath the sharp hairspray smell he caught a hint of something delicate.

She swayed back again. 'I'm *sure* it was you. The silly sisters were tittering with excitement, egging each other on to ask you to dance.'

'Silly sisters?'

'The other bridesmaids.'

'Ah.' No wonder she looked vaguely familiar. This was the bridesmaid who'd sat on the end of the long table, her dress of dark yellow tinged with green making her look slightly nauseous. Or maybe she *was* nauseous.

'Are you sick?'

'Only of the company in there.' Again those eyes grew huge and her hand hovered over her mouth.

Adoni watched, fascinated despite himself, as she blinked and stood straighter, the top of her head reaching the level of his mouth.

'It must be the champagne,' she murmured, her hand dropping. 'Who'd have thought it? I only had two glasses. Would that do it?' She tilted her head, surveying him owlishly.

'Do what?' Adoni repressed a smile.

'Make me so loqua...' Her brows knotted in concentration. 'Talkative. Normally I think before I speak. Always.'

He folded his arms over his chest. 'It depends how much you usually drink.'

'I don't. Tonight was my first taste of champagne.'

'Then yes, it probably is.' Diverted as he was, her friends would be looking for her. 'Isn't it time you went back?'

She shuddered and clutched his sleeve. 'No! Not till he's gone.' She looked at the controls. 'Why aren't we moving?' She slammed her hand onto the up button. 'I'm sorry. I hope you want to go up. I'll go anywhere so long as it's away from him.'

'The toad?'

'Yes! How did you know?' Her face broke into a wide smile that hit him in the solar plexus. When she smiled he saw something that even the plastered-on make-up couldn't conceal. 'Dark and brooding and clever too! I like you, Mr...?'

'Petrakis. Adoni Petrakis.'

Again those eyes rounded. 'Adoni?'

He nodded, waiting for the usual gushing excitement. He'd never had trouble attracting women but since he'd built his fortune...

'As in Adonis?'

'It's a Greek name.'

'Of course it is, but it's all wrong for you.' She squinted up at him, her lips pursed in a moue of concentration that looked surprisingly sexy, despite the bright shade of coral lipstick that clashed horribly with her pale skin. 'You're no Adonis.'

Adoni stared down at her. He was accustomed to flattery from women, not disappointment.

'You know who Adonis was?'

She waved a dismissive hand as if he interrupted her thought processes. 'In Greek mythology he was a gorgeous young man, loved by Aphrodite and later killed by a boar.' She bit her lip. 'Or maybe by someone else, I can't remember. But you're *not* an Adonis.'

Adoni couldn't keep his smile back. Had he ever met a woman who spoke to him like this? Not flattering and eager? 'Not pretty enough?'

Again that disparaging wave of her hand. 'No one could call you pretty.' Her voice rang with certainty. 'Handsome yes, but in a tough, dangerous sort of way. And those wicked eyebrows.' She lifted a hand towards his face but stopped short of touching him. 'More like Ares, god of war. Sexy but hard.'

The doors slid open behind her and she turned while Adoni was still trying to work out if he'd just been insulted or complimented.

'Oh, this is nice.' She drifted out of the lift into the foyer of his private suite, peering through the open door to the vast sitting room. 'Do you think it would be okay for me to stay here for a bit till he's gone?'

She moved forward, catching her shoe on the hand-knotted rug. Arms windmilling, she swayed till Adoni strode over and caught her upper arm. Her flesh was cool and smooth as silk.

'Are you sure you only had two glasses of champagne?'

She sagged against him, one hand planted on his chest. 'Absolutely. But I don't think I'd better have any more. I feel a little…different.' She blinked hazily up at him. 'Do *you* think I'm behaving oddly?'

What he thought was that, beneath the harsh make-up and the unflattering dress, this young woman was surprisingly appealing. And potentially vulnerable.

'Your friends will be missing you.'

She shook her head. 'Not my friends and they won't miss me. I don't know anyone there, except Emily—she's my cousin. And her parents. But they don't have time for me. They never did. I'm just a ring-in because bridesmaid number seven had to bail at the last minute. Oh, and the toad—I know him.' She grimaced. 'But I don't want to see him. Couldn't I just sit quietly for a bit? I could sneak out and catch a train home but I do feel a bit wobbly.'

Adoni scrutinised her. Clearly she couldn't make her way home alone yet. She was far too trusting to be let out without someone to keep an eye on her.

'Very well. Stay here and I'll make us coffee.'

'Lovely! I never thought of Ares being so domesticated. I think of him being all passion and fire.' She beamed again, that huge, beatific smile, and to his astonishment Adoni found himself smiling back. She was talking nonsense but her sense of humour appealed. As did the fact she didn't walk on eggshells around him.

'Do you think I could use the bathroom?'

'Of course. Down the corridor on the left.'

The sitting room was empty when Adoni came back. He set the tray of coffee and sweet shortbread on a table, telling himself he'd been a fool to let her in. He didn't know anything about her. Except that she couldn't hold her champagne and did know a surprising amount of Greek mythology. He didn't even know her name.

He stalked from the room, doubt rising. Where was she?

'Are you okay?' He pounded on the bathroom door.

'Sorry. I won't be long.'

'Are you sick?' She'd seemed tipsy, not drunk, but perhaps he was wrong.

'No. Not sick. Just sticky.'

Sticky? Adoni scowled. That made no sense.

The door opened and his visitor stepped out. She looked completely different. Shorter for a start, her shoes dangling from her hand.

'I used the shower. I feel much better now.' She stepped out into the corridor and tripped over the hem of her long dress, straight into his arms. Automatically Adoni caught her, but not before her soft breasts collided with his torso and her slim frame came to rest against him.

'Oops. Sorry.' She pulled back and smiled vaguely. 'This dress is too long. It was made for someone else.'

'Someone wearing shoes,' he murmured, trying to shove the thought of her lithe body from his mind.

'Ah.' She nodded. 'That explains it.' She sniffed. 'Is that coffee I smell?' Before he could answer she lifted her trailing skirt so high he caught a tantalising amount of shapely, bare legs before she turned and, hand on the wall, made her way to the sitting room.

Adoni took his time following. He'd been rocked by his response to the woman who'd emerged from the guest bathroom. Gone were the thick make-up and fake lashes. Without them he discovered a clear peaches and cream complexion that suited those dark blue eyes. Then there was a heart-shaped face and a pink mouth that looked too much like a cupid's bow for comfort.

Gone too was the elaborately curled and rigid hairstyle, threaded with mustard-yellow ribbon. Instead her dark hair lay straight and long around her shoulders. It was still wet, dripping at the ends, making the bodice of her dress water-stained and clingy.

He swallowed as he watched her turn and sink abruptly onto the sofa, the lamplight caressing the unexpectedly sweet tilt of her breast beneath the wet fabric. Heat stirred in his groin at the astounding sexual allure of her gentle curves and bare face.

Adoni frowned. His sex drive was healthy but such an instant, urgent response was rare. Especially as she wasn't even trying to attract him.

Was she?

He'd met some devious women in his time, going to extraordinary lengths to snare him, but instinct told him this one was exactly what she seemed.

'What's your name?' His voice emerged thick and abrupt but she didn't seem to notice.

'Alice. Alice Trehearn.' She looked over her shoulder at him and, to his astonishment, the line of her throat, the angle of her neat chin and the curve of her smile fanned the fire in his belly to a needy, urgent blast of heat.

'Don't frown, though I have to say you look very sexy when you do, all macho and...' Her words petered out and she squeezed her eyes shut. 'Remind me never to drink champagne again.'

Despite himself Adoni laughed. There was something so refreshing about a woman who spoke her mind.

'How old are you, Alice?' Suddenly it was important he find out.

'Twenty-three next week.' She turned away and poured milk into one of the coffees. 'How old are you?'

Relief filled him. With her unguarded behaviour he'd wondered if perhaps she was far younger. 'Thirty-one.'

A lifetime apart from her in experience, but, he realised in shock, that didn't dim his interest. His burgeoning interest. His trousers were too tight as he sat down opposite her.

'You look older.' She tilted her head as she surveyed him. 'Except when you smile. I like your smile. You should smile more often.' Carefully she put the milk jug down on the table.

Adoni's lips twitched. Had he really preferred candour? The answer was a definite yes.

'I thought you liked my...er...dark, brooding looks.'

'Oh, I do.' She stopped abruptly, her mouth sagging a little as if she realised what she'd said, then she focused on the mug of coffee, cautiously taking a sip. 'But your smile makes you look less like some bossy Greek god.'

'Ares?'

She nodded emphatically. 'Yes.' She paused. 'Or the one who threw thunderbolts.'

'Zeus?' Was he really so fearsome? Adoni preferred to think of himself as controlled and focused, a man who didn't suffer fools in business or gold-diggers in his personal life.

'That's the one.' Her brow furrowed. 'Except they always show him with a beard and you don't have one.'

Adoni suppressed a smile. 'I could grow one.'

'No.' She shook her head. 'That would be a waste. You've got a nice chin. Maybe a bit on the obstinate side but very nice.' She took another sip of coffee and smiled vaguely.

'Thank you. So do you.' It was a little pointed perhaps but just the right counterpoint for that lush mouth he found himself staring at.

Adoni leaned in and grabbed his mug, gulping hot coffee. When he lowered it, she was staring, her mouth slightly open and her breathing quick.

'Is everything all right?' He told himself he was behaving impeccably, pretending he didn't recognise her response for what it was—feminine interest. An answering interest quickened his pulse as he took in her delicate features and slim body.

'Fine. You just look so...'

Maybe she was sobering up, for she thought better of finishing her comment.

'So...?' Adoni didn't fish for compliments but he found himself wondering what she'd been about to say.

Dark lashes veiled her eyes as she took another sip of coffee. 'Nice. You look nice.'

He'd bet his last dollar that wasn't what she'd been going to say. 'You do too.'

'There's no need to lie.' She lifted her head, viewing him from under regally arched eyebrows. 'I look dreadful. Why Emily chose this colour I don't know. Honestly, it's the colour of baby poo.'

Adoni laughed. She was right; it was reminiscent of a rather nasty stain. 'It's fair to say it's not a good match for your colouring.'

'That's what *I* said, but it was too late to change it. Too late even to alter the fit.' Her mouth turned down in a sulky pout Adoni found far too seductive.

'At least it's only for one night.'

She nodded. 'That's what I keep telling myself. It's a day of firsts.'

'Firsts?'

Another nod. 'Absolutely. First time wearing yellow, for one thing. Never again.' She shuddered. 'First time in London. First time as a bridesmaid. I thought it would be a lot more fun but the other bridesmaids kept tittering and gossiping amongst themselves. And the groomsmen...'

'Not your type?'

She shrugged hugely and one pillowy puffed sleeve slid off her shoulder. 'I don't really know. But I think not.' She lifted her legs and tucked them under her then wriggled back on the sofa.

There shouldn't have been anything remotely seductive about the action yet Adoni found himself fixated on that luscious little shimmy of hips and breasts.

'You don't know?' His voice sounded unfamiliar.

She shook her head. 'I need to research more.' She blinked back at him and smiled. 'I have some firsts.' She looked down at her dress and scowled. 'But there are a lot of nevers too.'

'Nevers?' Adoni's English was excellent but he'd never heard of that before.

'Absolutely.' She lifted one finger. 'Never had luck with the opposite sex.' Then a second finger. 'Never had a kiss that blew my socks off.' Her gaze narrowed. 'You look like a man who could blow a girl's socks off with a kiss.'

Adoni choked on his coffee. 'Is that a proposition?' He was torn between amusement and a dark, fast-running channel of temptation.

Devoid of that tacky lipstick, Alice Trehearn had the most alluring mouth he'd ever seen. He swallowed hard and reminded himself this was the drink talking.

'As if a man like you would kiss a girl like me.' She leaned her head back against the sofa, her eyelids drooping. She lapsed into silence and he wondered if she was falling asleep.

'Never driven a car either.' She sighed. 'I bet you have a *lovely* car.'

'Yes, I do.' And there was no way he was letting this inebriated woman near it, despite her eager smile. 'But I'm not letting you drive it.'

She looked so ridiculously disappointed, her mouth turning down at the edges, that he almost wished he could bring back that sunny smile of hers and the twinkle in her fine eyes.

'Is there anything else on your never list?'

Alice opened her mouth then closed it again. A flush of pink rose to her cheeks. Instantly his interest piqued.

'Alice?'

She shook her head. 'It's nothing.' She leaned forward, reached for her coffee and, seeing the mug empty, sank back.

'You might as well tell me what it is you haven't done. I promise to keep it to myself.'

Was he really so curious about her?

To his surprise, Adoni discovered he was.

She fidgeted. 'I'm doing all the talking. Shouldn't you tell *me* something?' Just as if she hadn't barged uninvited into his private suite. Yet Adoni hadn't enjoyed a woman's conversation so much in a long time.

What did that say about the women he dated?

'What do you want me to say?'

She shrugged, melting even further into the sofa. 'Anything you like. Tell me something you haven't told anyone else. I promise to keep it to myself.'

The idea was absurd. Why share with a complete stranger? Yet as he sat in the mellow lamplight, watching Alice Trehearn's easy smile and expectant look, he found himself tempted.

Because he wasn't accustomed to sharing anything truly personal?

Because she was a stranger he'd never see again?

That, and the surprising tug of attraction, must be why he even considered playing along. And why he'd allowed her into his space when he was notoriously private.

His mood had been odd all evening. Restlessness had kept him on edge. Remarkably, it was only since she'd inserted herself into his presence that he'd begun to relax.

'I don't like weddings.' The words came suddenly. Adoni was surprised how good it felt to admit it.

'Really?' One fine eyebrow arched. 'Any particular reason?'

He took another mouthful of coffee. It didn't taste as rich this time. 'I was nearly married once. I suppose weddings bring back memories.'

Of rejection, disbelief and disappointment. But he'd been young enough to learn his lesson well. These days, apart from his hand-picked managers, he didn't put his trust in anyone but himself. It was safer that way. When those closest to you could turn so viciously against you, trust was the first casualty, along with love.

Absently he rolled his shoulder, releasing a stiffness along the collarbone.

'I'm so sorry.' She leaned forward, her hand lifted towards him as if to smooth away the frown he felt settle on his brow. Then she sank back, regarding him seriously.

He waited for the inevitable, a question about why his marriage hadn't proceeded, but again Alice Trehearn surprised him. Even inebriated she had enough delicacy not to trespass further. 'Tonight must have been a trial.'

He shook his head, automatically rejecting sympathy. 'It was fine. It was no big deal.' Time to change the subject. 'So what is the other thing you've never done? I told you my secret. It's time for you to share too.'

She blinked, staring back at him with a look he couldn't interpret. Annoyance? Embarrassment? Certainly the colour in her cheeks warmed to rose madder.

'Alice?'

Her mouth tightened and then the words tumbled out. 'Never had an orgasm, if you must know.' For an instant she looked as regal as a young swan, stretching her neck higher and tilting her chin, trying to hide what he guessed was embarrassment.

Then something unexpected flashed in her eyes. 'I don't suppose you'd like to help me with that?'

CHAPTER TWO

HELP HER HAVE her first orgasm? Adoni tried and failed over the next hour to put Alice Trehearn's words from his mind.

The idea was so outrageous it was laughable.

A woman, clearly the worse for drink, propositioning him so clumsily.

A woman without glamour or any of the usual seductive skills he expected in a lover.

A woman in an ill-fitting dress the colour of bile, with her hair hanging damp around her shoulders and not a scrap of make-up. She didn't belong in his world and shouldn't be in the least attractive.

Yet Adoni couldn't banish the provocative idea of giving Alice her first orgasm.

Was it the idea of initiating her to pleasure that snared his imagination and wouldn't let go? Or was it Alice herself?

The rose-pink colour of her cheeks would spread across her breasts. Those dark eyes would glitter and that decadent mouth would open on a gasp, or perhaps a scream as he toppled her over the edge into rapture.

The image of her naked beneath him, trembling with satiation, was so vivid it had him rock-hard in an instant.

The chirp of his phone, an urgent call from his North American manager, had saved both him and Alice from the embarrassment of a response. Then, when he'd ended the call and turned to tell her she needed to leave since he had work to do, Adoni had found her asleep.

Suspicious, he'd initially wondered if it was a ploy, especially as she looked ridiculously cute curled up, hands beneath her cheek and bare feet pale against the cushions.

But her occasional tiny snuffles proved him wrong. They were too close to dainty snores for any would-be seductress to countenance.

Now, sitting at his desk on the other side of the room, reviewing the contract his manager had just sent, Adoni directed a darkling stare towards the woman lying on his sofa.

How dare she make such an invitation then go to sleep? She rolled onto her back, the too-big bodice pulling askew to reveal the gentle curve of one pale breast.

The pulse in Adoni's groin pounded hard and fast as his gaze traced her slender figure. His mouth dried as she shifted and the edge of the fabric strained, close to revealing one nipple. Her skirt was rucked up above her knees from the way she'd twisted. Even so, most of her was covered by that appalling bridesmaid's dress.

She shouldn't look attractive, much less seductive. Yet Adoni registered the heaviness in his lower body, the restlessness, the powerful hunger.

Maybe it was that sultry mouth, those lush, slightly downturned lips, surely designed for sin. He looked at her and thought of those lips on his body and it was no wonder he couldn't concentrate on the document before him.

Perhaps it was the novelty of not knowing what she was going to say next. Her cheerfully frank assessment of how she looked in that dreadful dress, or the apparently artless combination of guilelessness and insight.

Or was it the shy hints that she wanted him? The blush, the spark in her eye when she'd asked about him giving her an orgasm.

Of all the preposterous pick-up lines, that was the best he'd heard.

Except it hadn't been a pick-up line. She hadn't wanted to admit her inexperience. That probably explained her flippant question about him helping her rid herself of that particular lack in her life. She'd been bluffing. Of course she had.

Adoni turned back to the screen. Yet it wasn't the legal document he saw, but the rosy blush that coloured her creamy skin and her haughty, challenging glare.

Give her an orgasm? The trouble was how much the idea enticed.

What had she said? She'd never had luck with men, never had a kiss that knocked her socks off. Never had an orgasm. Clearly she *was* unlucky if none of her lovers had bothered to take care of that when they sought their own pleasure.

Adoni's heart might no longer be engaged when he had sex, but he prided himself on being a generous lover. His partner's satisfaction added to his own pleasure, and he'd no more bed a woman and leave her wanting than he'd renege on a business contract.

The contract. He ploughed his fingers through his hair, sinking his head into his hands and forcing his attention back to the computer.

He'd finish the contract then wake Ms Trouble-on-Two-Legs Trehearn and send her off in a taxi. Then he'd get a decent night's sleep ready for work tomorrow, despite it being Sunday.

Adoni ground his teeth at the sly voice telling him his life was lacking if that was the best he could do on a Saturday night. Send home the female he lusted after then get an early night ready for work.

Was this what all those years of toil had been for? He'd scraped himself up from the gutter when Vassili Petrakis, the man he'd believed to be his father, disowned him. He'd risen above the pain of his fiancée's rejection and poured his anger and determination into building his company from nothing.

He'd let his drive to succeed fill the void where his personal life used to be. He had no family to distract him now.

Fleetingly, he thought of his younger brothers, a pang of regret piercing his chest. But they belonged to another life, one barred to him for ever.

Now he was CEO of a company worth billions. He had homes in Greece and the UK, plus a ski chalet in Colorado and a yacht that shared its time between the Med and the Caribbean. Not that he managed much downtime to enjoy them.

Adoni sighed and raked his hand through his hair again. Maybe that was the problem. He needed a vacation.

Or an affair. Intense, enjoyable and short—just the way he liked them. He had no inclination for long-term now he'd taught himself never to trust a woman's intentions, despite protests of undying love.

Rubbing his temples, he hunched over the screen, re-reading clauses he'd skimmed half a dozen times.

He was just sending his response to his New York manager when the back of his neck prickled. He stiffened, instantly aware that his guest was awake. He felt her eyes on him. Worse, that needy throb in his groin was back full force, reminding him he'd been celibate longer than usual.

Even so his reaction to this woman was unprecedented.

Adoni didn't turn to look at her. That would, for reasons he couldn't identify, be a sign of weakness. Instead he finished his message, sent it, then closed the computer. Only then did he deign to swivel round in his seat.

She was standing, half turned from him. The satin of her dress slid over svelte, sinuous curves and delectably long legs as she raised her hands to fix her hair in a tight knot.

'Don't.' The sound of his voice surprised him and made her swing round, eyes wide. 'I like it down.'

He couldn't read her expressive eyes from this distance but the sudden clamp of her jaw made him expect some dismissive response.

Adoni was surprised when, instead, she paused, arms still raised. 'Do you?'

When he nodded she dropped her arms and a dark curtain of hair fell to cloak her shoulders. Now it was dry he saw rich hints of auburn in the dark brown. He curled his hands closed against the impulse to get up and stroke those shimmering tresses.

Her breasts rose with her deep breath and Adoni's gaze trailed from her bare shoulder where one sleeve drooped down her arm, across the upper slope of her breasts then up via her slender throat to her lips.

Damn! That sulky, sexy mouth would be the death of common sense. Why hadn't he fully appreciated it till she wiped the horrible lipstick away?

'I'm sorry. I didn't mean to fall asleep on your sofa.' Had she misinterpreted his shudder of arousal for one of disdain? 'I apologise for...' she faltered and gestured wide '...for inviting myself in here.' She looked around the vast executive suite as if she'd never seen it. Presumably she hadn't taken in her surroundings earlier.

That, and the way she spoke, plus the shadow of tension where before there'd been nothing but a lack of inhibition, told Adoni the effects of the alcohol were wearing off.

He was torn between relief that she was obviously recovered enough to go home, and regret.

As if he wanted her to stay.

For her amusing conversation, or something else?

White teeth bit that plump bottom lip. Did she read the sexual interest he couldn't douse?

'No need to apologise. It's been an interesting evening.'

She shut her eyes for a moment. 'I'm sure it has. You've been very forbearing. Thank you for...' again that wave of one hand '...for the coffee and for letting me sleep.' Once again, soft colour stained her pale cheeks. Adoni found himself wondering how long it had been since he'd met a woman who still blushed.

'My pleasure.' He stood and again her eyes rounded as they traced him, as if she hadn't realised how tall he was. Or perhaps he looked different now he'd shed his jacket and tie, undone a couple of buttons and rolled up his sleeves.

Neither moved. Did he imagine the heavy chug of energy thickening the atmosphere? Adoni wasn't prone to flights of fancy, yet it seemed all the air in the room was being sucked away, making it hard to breathe.

He watched her swallow, her slender throat pale and alluring, especially when compared with that mustard horror of a dress. It was as if someone had taken something pure and hidden it beneath layers of camouflage.

Pure? An old-fashioned word for a woman who'd blatantly invited him to be sexually intimate. Yet it seemed apt. Alice Trehearn was surely the most honest woman he'd ever met. In Adoni's world, where people pretended affection in return for material comforts, honesty was the purest quality he knew.

He took a step closer and Alice's insides twisted like a riot of butterflies dipping and fluttering over a spring meadow.

Now the effects of the wine had worn off she was stunned to find herself alone with such a man.

That he was wealthy and powerful went without saying. It was obvious from the casual way he wore his hand-tailored clothes and the equally nonchalant way he took this exquisite, ultra-expensive suite for granted.

But it wasn't the fact he came from a world far removed from her own that made her stare. It was the man himself. Tall, with a hard, chiselled face that had more than a trace of arrogance in those winged black eyebrows and high cheekbones. His mouth looked as if it didn't smile enough, as if his world was too serious. Yet when he did smile his eyes, an amazing colour somewhere between blue and green, danced. The tight curve of his lips undid her as if he reached out and loosened a ribbon deep inside her.

What on earth had she said to him? She remembered some of their conversation, not all. She vividly recalled his laugh, rich and warm, enfolding her.

He hadn't laughed *at* her, despite her appearance and the way the wine affected her. He'd laughed *with* her, sharing whatever joke she'd made. That sense of humour undercut her common sense. It was too appealing.

How she'd missed laughter lately.

She felt a link to this man she'd never experienced before, except to David, her godfather, who'd been her best friend despite the age difference. But her feelings for David had been a far cry from *this*. She swallowed hard, simultaneously shocked and intrigued by the way her body came alive under the Greek's sea-bright stare. Tiny shivers prickled her skin and her nipples budded against the loose bodice of her dress.

When he noticed, his gaze dropping to her breasts, Alice's breath clogged and excitement danced in her blood. To her amazement her breasts seemed to both tighten and swell. She'd never felt anything like it. But then her experience of men, and of sexual arousal, was almost zero.

She blinked, lifting her hands to rub her bare arms.

Was she trying to invite his attention? As if he'd be interested in a woman so ordinary and unsophisticated!

Yet her feet seemed welded to the floor.

'Well, thank you again for your hospitality.' She moistened her bottom lip with her tongue and was shocked when his eyes zeroed in on the movement. A hot wire of sensation tugged between her mouth and her breasts, then down to the achy spot between her legs. 'I should be going.'

She made herself turn, looking for her handbag on the sofa. When she turned back he was closer—much closer.

She had to tilt her head back to keep eye contact. Dimly she realised she was barefoot, that she'd need to search for her shoes. Her toes curled into the thick pile of the rug at the look in his eyes.

'Is someone waiting for you at home?'

Alice frowned, feeling the sudden gnaw of anxiety that had become so familiar. She'd lost her home when David died and, though she'd known that day would come, she'd been so caught up in looking after him, making his final days comfortable, she hadn't focused enough on where she'd live afterwards. Her little nest egg hadn't gone nearly as far as she'd hoped. Nest egg! It had been barely enough to keep a roof over her head until she got a job.

'I live alone.'

'Then there's no rush to leave.' Those sleek dark eyebrows rose as his expression turned wickedly seductive.

Alice's heart banged her ribs and her breath stalled. 'Are you...' She paused, hardly crediting what she read in his face. 'Are you suggesting I stay here?'

'You weren't so hesitant earlier.' His smile was slow and intense and it superheated her blood.

'I wasn't?'

He frowned. 'You don't remember?'

'I...' She frowned as snippets of conversation came back to her in vivid clarity. 'I asked if you were a good kisser.' Part of her shrank at the memory of such champagne-induced frankness, but now she was here, toe to toe with this fascinating man, excitement overrode bashfulness.

'Would you still like to find out?' His voice dropped to a low note that wound its way through her belly and down to her knees, making them wobble.

Impossible that he should affect her so intensely, this man whose name she couldn't even recall. Adoni something. She knew so little about him.

Sensible Alice Trehearn, the one who'd spent years being

dependable, devoted and reliable, knew this was her cue to leave. Yet another Alice Trehearn, the one who secretly yearned for *life*, and who'd only surfaced previously in her hell-for-leather gallops across the moor, shivered in excitement.

'Yes.' The word was out before she thought about it. Because if she thought about it she'd never say it.

'Good,' he murmured. 'Your mouth has been driving me crazy.'

Her mouth? Alice lifted a hand to her lips but instead met his chin as his head lowered. He stopped a breath away. She felt his exhalation on her lips, scented with coffee and brandy and something indefinable. The pads of her fingers trembled against the solid plane of his jaw, then spread, testing warm skin with a hint of stubble that grazed her flesh as she settled her whole palm across his chin.

She'd shaved both her father and later her godfather, David, when each grew too ill to do it themselves. Neither had been like this. Adoni radiated heat and vigour and a sensuality she felt right down to the marrow in her bones. He was strong, his flesh taut and so vitally *alive*.

Alice drew a shuddering breath filled with the alien, delicious scent of man in his prime. She stared up into eyes as bright as she imagined the Aegean Sea to be. She read a question there. He was giving her time to change her mind.

In answer, Alice slid her hand around into his thick, short dark hair, surprised at its softness. She rose on tiptoe and pressed her lips to his.

For a moment he didn't move and she cringed inside. This was a mistake. Hadn't she known he couldn't really be interested?

Then his mouth moved on hers, gently persuading her lips apart. His warm tongue slicked her lips then delved within and everything inside her melted and swayed at the eroticism of that sweet invasion. Her belly liquefied, her knees loosened and it was only the firm loop of his arm around her waist that kept her high against him.

His other hand eased the hair back from her face in a gesture so tender her heart rolled over.

Alice slipped her other hand up over his chest. The feel of hard, lean muscle sent a sizzle of excitement through her. She leaned closer, a willing pupil as he delved deeper, drawing out the kiss into something that sent shivery hot darts of flame through her blood.

She didn't know which was better—the way Adoni kissed, making her feel treasured, or the feel of their bodies locked tight. The arm at her waist slid lower, drawing her hips against him.

Her breath stilled as she came in contact with a hard length against her belly.

Instantly he lifted his mouth and Alice almost wailed with disappointment at her loss, her face instantly tilting higher as if to tempt him back. Instead he pressed his lips to her forehead.

A shudder racked his tall frame and it hit her that she wasn't the only one swept away in the moment. Surprise and satisfaction filled her. Even if this had started as a one-sided favour it had become something else.

'Adoni?' Her voice was husky and uneven.

He drew back just far enough to meet her eyes. What did he see? She felt flushed and wanton, not like herself.

'This is your chance to change your mind.' Gone was the slightly teasing gleam she'd seen in his face when he'd talked of kissing her. Now he looked solemn to the point of grimness.

'About kissing you?'

'And the rest of what you wanted.'

The rest? Her brow furrowed as she tried to recall their earlier conversation but her foggy memory couldn't compete with the heady sensations bombarding her. That delicious spicy scent of his skin, the rich flavour of him still on her tongue. The heat of his large body surrounding her and that strange mix of vulnerability and power she felt at the differences in their closely aligned bodies.

'You wanted an orgasm.'

Fire flooded her face as she met his steady scrutiny.

'Please, tell me I didn't say that.'

One corner of that thin mouth tipped up and fire trailed through her middle right down to her womb.

'Apparently the men you've known haven't been very obliging.'

Alice closed her eyes and dropped her forehead against his collarbone. Maybe if she wished hard enough she'd wake up in her own bed and discover this was a dream.

An intense, remarkably erotic dream. One large palm circled her lower back and instinctively her pelvis tilted forward, right to that hard column of masculine arousal.

Should she tell him there'd been no men in her life, not the way he thought? Admit that her previous experience of kissing had been once in her early teens and once again a couple of years ago, neither of them memorable except for her disappointment. Clearly her expectations had been too high.

But this man blasted those expectations to smithereens. She'd never thought a kiss could make her feel so...

'Alice?'

She lifted her head. 'I'd like to kiss you again.' Her voice was rough, unrecognisable, and she swiped her tongue over her bottom lip. A shudder ripped through her at the way his eyes narrowed on the movement.

'Is that all you want?'

She opened her mouth but didn't know what to say. She'd never had a conversation like this. She'd assumed that when the time was right and she'd finally found a man with whom she wanted to lose her virginity, it would just...happen.

Stupid to be shy now when she'd apparently already propositioned the guy. But now she was sober. Her head as clear as it was possible to be when wrapped in the arms of an impossibly gorgeous Greek God of a man.

'Couldn't we just kiss and see what happens?'

Again that tiny uptilt to the corner of his mouth, only this time Alice read tension there as much as humour. 'I already know what will happen. We'll have sex and we won't stop till we're both utterly sated.'

Her heart gave a wild flutter and something tugged hard inside her. She felt moisture at her core and wriggled, hyper-aware that the ribbon of fabric between her legs was damp.

'You need to decide.'

He gave her the choice to step away and behave like sensible, sane Alice Trehearn.

Yet how could she when the tips of his fingers traced a pattern of temptation across her back? They roved from one hip to the other, dipping and swirling and making desire course through her.

'I...' She closed her eyes, trying to gather her wits. But all she could summon was the realisation she wanted this man as she'd never wanted before. It didn't matter that she'd always imagined sex as part of a loving, committed relationship. Life had taught her that you never knew what was around the corner and happiness had to be grabbed with both hands.

Maybe it was partly the champagne but she sensed it was Adoni himself who tempted her to take a step she'd never taken before.

Surely he was the perfect man to initiate her into sexual pleasure?

What did she have to lose except her inexperience?

And wouldn't a night in his bed be the perfect antidote to loneliness? Loneliness had compounded the sharp ache of grief since she'd been forced to leave David's estate and all the people she cared for.

Firm hands gripped her shoulders and he stepped back, shocking Alice with the sudden, urgent distress she felt.

'No! Don't!' She looked up into those dazzling eyes and knew there was only one answer she could give if she was to be true to herself. 'I can't guarantee orgasms but I'd like to stay with you.' The words came out in a breathless tumble.

A warm hand cupped her chin, his thumb stroking rhythmically over her mouth till her bottom lip dropped open and Adoni traced her mouth. Alice shivered at the heavy weight of desire filling her belly and the decadent promise of pleasure in his remarkable eyes.

'I'd like you to stay too, Alice.' The way he said her name, with the slightest of accents, sent a shiver of pleasure through her. 'As for the orgasms—' he smiled, a slow, sexy smile '—let me worry about those.'

CHAPTER THREE

ADONI ROLLED ONTO his back, his blood thundering, after-shocks of rapture echoing through him. Light flashed in the blackness of his closed eyes and he struggled for breath, his chest rising mightily as he sucked in air.

Finally he found the strength to open his eyes and stare at the ceiling of his bedroom. It looked unfamiliar, as if the events of the evening had changed his perspective, even on something as mundane as cream paint.

Certainly he felt different. Not just sated but as if he'd tapped into an energy source that both drained and renewed him at the same time.

'They didn't do it right,' he said finally, his voice raw.

'Sorry?' Alice's voice was a wisp of sound. It shivered across pleasure points on his body that were still remarkably receptive to that sweet cadence.

'The guys you had sex with. The ones who didn't give you an orgasm. They had no idea what they were doing.'

For Alice Trehearn had to be one of the most sensual women he'd met. Her responsiveness, her passion, had soldered a connection between them that felt rare, almost precious, even if her limited experience had been glaringly obvious. She hadn't been able to conceal her shock at some of his caresses.

At one stage, when he'd finally allowed himself to thrust deep within her, he'd even imagined for a moment that he was her first. She was so incredibly taut and close around him she might have been a virgin. Except virgins didn't offer themselves to strangers and talk so casually of orgasms.

He'd half wondered if, despite her frank talking, she

might be reticent and cold with a man. Instead she'd been like a live wire just waiting to explode in a shower of sparks.

Aware that she'd never before had an orgasm, Adoni had taken his time exploring her body, lavishing caresses all over till she was trembling and gasping against him, sobbing for release. Her throaty pleas had been sweet as wild honey and had prolonged her sensual torture. For he'd lingered, experimenting, revelling in each gasped exclamation.

By the time he'd slipped his fingers across that nub at the centre of her need, it had taken barely a caress for her to lift off the bed, shuddering as she gasped out her release. And again when he'd nuzzled her there...

Adoni closed his eyes at the vivid memory of musk and sweet femininity, of silky thighs clamping round him and her choked little cries of disbelief as rapture took her.

He'd almost come undone there and then, so aroused was he by this woman. Yet she'd been worth the wait. Finding his own completion, deep-seated within her velvet heat, watching her slate-blue eyes blaze in wonder as her body reached that pinnacle a third time. That was a pleasure that would stay with him well into the future. He couldn't remember another climax so intense it felt as if he'd lost a part of himself.

But he'd eagerly lose himself again and again with a lover like Alice Trehearn. Even now, gasping for breath as they fought their way down from that incredible high, her fingers splayed possessively across his thigh.

If this was how it was when they barely knew each other's bodies, what would it be like when they were even better attuned?

How would it feel if she did for him some of the things he'd done for her?

Adrenaline slammed into his blood, hurtling around his body at dangerous speeds.

'Well, I'm glad *you* know what you're doing.' Her voice was an uneven whisper. 'That was amazing.'

Something about the hoarse strain in her tone made Adoni open his eyes and turn his head.

She too lay on her back, staring at the ceiling, her pert breasts rising and falling with her rapid breathing. The sight of them, the memory of their sweetness on his tongue, sent a charge of energy back to his groin.

Again? So soon?

Adoni smiled, his nostrils flaring as he inhaled the scent of sex underlain with the orange blossom fragrance of her hair. There was something overwhelmingly attractive about a woman who made a man feel all man.

He opened his mouth to murmur something suggestive when his gaze rose to her face and his mouth snapped shut.

Her pale brow was furrowed in thought and those full lips pursed as if something other than bliss occupied her brain. His gaze moved to a reddened patch of skin on her slender throat. Razor burn. He'd kissed her there as he powered into her, stifling the need to yell his triumphant pleasure with a ravaging caress of her tender flesh.

'Alice?'

She blinked rapidly and to Adoni's consternation he saw fat tears spike her dark lashes.

He didn't do emotion. Not with lovers. Sex was about pleasure, scratching an itch, not—

Her tongue slipped out to swipe her reddened lips and, despite his sudden tension, Adoni's sex stirred.

'Sorry.' She swiped her cheeks with the heel of her palm. 'I'm feeling a little…overwhelmed. It will pass, I'm sure.' Her laugh sounded strained. 'It was just so much more than I expected.'

She turned her head and snared him with her brilliant eyes. Adoni's heart knocked his ribs in a rough, unfamiliar rhythm.

'Thank you.' Her mouth turned up into a crooked smile that did something devastating to his internal organs.

'My pleasure.' What a weird conversation. They were so…polite when just seconds ago he'd been deep within her, pulsing out his climax and revelling in her broken gasps of wonderment and the close embrace of her body.

He wanted to kiss her again, see if the promising stirrings of his lower body would strengthen. But that mouth was so solemn. That puckered brow so serious. Above all, there were those crystal teardrops clinging to her thick, bunched lashes. Those made him pause and rethink.

'I need to see to the condom.' Even as he said it, an inner voice rose in protest, telling him he could have her again, find easy satisfaction with this unlikely siren.

But a lifetime's caution came to his aid. He refused to get involved with feminine tears and…feelings.

He levered himself from the bed and strode across to the bathroom. Strange how, with every step, he felt the weight of her gaze. It was as if she touched him, a light caress that strayed from his shoulders, down the sweep of his spine to his buttocks and thighs, then back up to the bunching muscles of his glutes. A shiver of awareness rippled through him.

Again, temptation rose to turn back to Alice and take more of what they'd already shared. Instead Adoni kept walking. It was only when he closed the bathroom door behind him that the tension pushing at his shoulders eased.

In the end he decided on a cold shower, sluicing water off his face and relying on the chill to douse his libido. It would be too easy to fall back into sex with Alice Trehearn. Her combination of naivety and forthright ways attracted as he couldn't recall being attracted before. She was different, possibly unique, and something about her cut straight through his hard-won caution to the instinctive risk-taker deep within.

Which was why Adoni would take stock before having sex with her again.

That they *would* have sex again was a certainty. He might be cautious but he wasn't a self-denying fool.

He grabbed a towel, roughly drying his hair, then leaned forward, considering the shadow darkening his jaw. He should shave, out of consideration for Alice's delicate skin. Yet he hesitated. He'd gone blindly into sex with a stranger and got more than he'd bargained for, in satisfaction and pleasure. But in tears too, and that made the hackles of caution rise.

For a second he hesitated. That in itself piqued his anger. He prided himself on his quick decisions, yet with this woman he was second guessing. Frowning, he reached for a towel and wrapped it around his hips. They had some talking to do.

After that there'd be time for shaving and for more sex. Lots more sex.

Adoni repressed the urge to smile as he crossed the vast bathroom. Already he was fantasising about where the next time would be. The whole time he'd showered he'd been picturing Alice naked with him under the icy spray. Or naked on the sofa by the fire. Or up against the big picture window that gave his owner's suite its multi-million-dollar views of central London.

He swallowed, his mouth drying as he thought of those delectable legs wrapped around his waist, her sultry mouth open as she gasped her pleasure and—

Adoni slammed to a stop. The sheets were a riotous tumble on the vast, empty bed but Alice wasn't beneath them. He frowned.

Was that a door he heard closing down the corridor?

'Alice?' He cast about, expecting to see her in some dim corner of the room, but she wasn't there. Nor was that abomination of a dress.

A niggling sensation started up in his belly. He couldn't place it but it reminded him of the nerves he'd felt the first time he'd gone, virtually penniless, to beg for a loan to start his business. When he'd had nothing to recommend him but his bright ideas and determination to succeed or die trying. Anything to prove to Vassili Petrakis that the son he'd disinherited was a man to be reckoned with.

The memory of that day halted him, mid-stride. His frown became a scowl. Nothing could compare to the way he'd felt that day.

Yet that curious, unsettled feeling persisted.

His stride lengthened as he headed down the corridor, checking out each room as he went. She was nowhere to be found. He paced the sitting room. Hadn't she left her shoes beside the couch? Hadn't her purse been there too?

'Alice?' He swung round, taking in the unmistakable emptiness.

She'd gone. Not just gone, but run away without a word. Unbelievable! No woman had ever done that before.

He didn't like it.

Adoni retraced his steps, his brow furrowed as he tried to work out why she'd run.

Embarrassment? It seemed unlikely, given the conversation they'd had and her enthusiasm for sex. Heat stirred anew at the memory of Alice, abandoned with rapture. It had felt like the first *real* moment in this long, trying day. He'd even had someone trying to sell him real estate over the wedding dinner.

Adoni stood in the bedroom doorway, scanning the room as if it could provide a clue to her bizarre behaviour. In his experience women were far more likely to hang around long after you wished they'd left than go too early. Most had that greedy look in their eyes. The one that said they lusted after his body or his money or probably both.

Unease filled him. Was Alice capable of looking after

herself alone in London late at night? Should he follow her?
She wasn't drunk any more, he'd never have taken her to
bed if she was, but—

His thoughts halted as he spied his wallet on the floor.
When he'd shed his clothes it had still been in the pocket
of his trousers. Now it lay, splayed open, beside the bed.
The side of the bed where Alice had lain, exhausted and
emotional.

Apparently exhausted and emotional. For now he stepped
closer Adoni saw that not only was his wallet open but one
of his credit cards was tugged out of its slot.

He blinked, mind cataloguing the implication of the open
wallet. Yet something, a part of him that hankered after the
illusion of an honest woman, protested he couldn't be seeing what he thought.

Adoni picked up the wallet and sank onto the bed. How
much cash had been in there earlier? He flicked through
the notes. Nothing was obviously missing. But that didn't
mean she hadn't helped herself to some.

Of more concern was that she'd obviously been rifling
his credit cards. They were all there; she hadn't stolen them.

But maybe she'd made a note of the numbers and security data to use later? She could even have taken an imprint.
Who knew what she carried in her bag?

Adoni leaned back against the bedhead, torn between
disbelief and anger at himself for being so easily gulled.
Women had tried to inveigle their way into his life in so
many ways, he'd thought himself awake to them all. Yet
he'd allowed Alice Trehearn to slip under his guard.

If that was even her name. Now he thought about it, it
sounded a little too sweet and old-fashioned. Made up to
allay suspicion?

He raked a hand through his hair. What a bloody fool
he'd been! Thinking with his penis while she'd been busy
scheming to get her grimy fingers on his money.

You'd think, by thirty-one, he'd be awake to such schemes. Especially given his history. A mother who'd lied shamelessly to both her husband and her son. A fiancée who'd fooled Adoni into believing she loved him then dropped him the moment he was disinherited.

As for the man he'd once called Father...

Truly, it was remarkable Adoni had allowed himself to be conned. He'd learned the hard way not to take people at face value.

Until tonight when a slip of a girl with an endearing smile, an owlish stare and a voracious sensuality had blindsided him.

His mind clicked back to that heady rush of primal, masculine possessiveness. That first slow thrust to Alice's silken core, when she'd felt as tight and untried as he imagined a virgin would be. Then she'd looked up with wonder in her glazed eyes and something had beaten hard and insistent in his chest. Pleasure and a primitive satisfaction that made him feel as sophisticated as a caveman.

He'd even believed, when her breath caught and her whole body stilled, that perhaps she *was* a complete innocent. Until her fingers dug into his buttocks and she demanded 'More!' in that husky little voice that was the most potent aphrodisiac he knew. That had banished the strange moment of fantasy.

Adoni's jaw set. He supposed he should be thankful he hadn't taken longer in the bathroom. If he had he was sure his wallet and his credit cards would have been exactly where he'd left them and he wouldn't have realised Alice was a thief till large sums disappeared from his accounts.

Alice Trehearn was just another gold-digger who'd set her sights on his fortune.

He breathed out hard, shoulders rising and falling in self-disgust that he'd actually fallen for her scam. She'd better look out if their paths crossed again. He wouldn't fall for her wiles a second time.

He reached for the phone. It was time to cancel his credit cards.

'Sensitive breasts. That was the first sign.' The woman's whisper penetrated the hum of the crowded café. 'Even when I just crossed my arms.'

Alice paused, feeling her eyes widen at the empty cups and plates she was clearing from a nearby table. Her own breasts had felt sensitive for the last couple of days.

Out of all the customer conversations in the room, her tired brain *would* snag on that one. Any minute now she'd hear that the woman had since been diagnosed with a weird flu or some horrible life-threatening illness. Alice did *not* need to hear that. She couldn't afford time off with illness. She had enough trouble making ends meet.

She blinked and tried to focus on her task, wrinkling her nose at the half-drunk coffee she loaded onto her tray. For some reason the scent of coffee, one she usually adored, seemed downright unpleasant today.

'I didn't have that at all.' Another woman spoke. 'My first sign was cigarette smoke. Every time Jake lit up I gagged. I made him quit smoking, which is just as well when you think about it. But it wasn't just cigarettes. Coffee too. I couldn't bear the smell.'

Alice froze, her arm outstretched towards a cake plate.

Was this some hoax? Was she being set up in an elaborate joke?

She shook her head. Tiredness was confusing her. She'd spoken to no one about either of those strange symptoms. It was just coincidence.

Briskly, telling herself she wasn't listening, she finished stacking the tray.

'And of course that led to morning sickness.' It was the

second voice again. 'You don't know how lucky you were to miss out on that.'

Alice felt the hairs on her nape lift, one by one, till her flesh drew tight. She took a slow, calming breath, its effect spoiled as another waitress walked by with a load of coffees. Alice inhaled the fumes and swallowed convulsively.

She felt clammy now, as if her skin was too tight for her body. Perspiration popped out on her hairline and she swayed.

It took an enormous effort to straighten, supporting the laden tray, and turn towards the kitchen. As she did her gaze turned to the pair who'd been speaking. Both were young and healthy-looking. Both smiling. One had a baby on her knee and the other was so pregnant it was a wonder she managed to fit in the alcove seat.

A tremor racked Alice and she almost dropped the tray.

Pregnancy!

That was what they were talking about?

But Alice couldn't be. It wasn't possible.

He'd used a condom!

Of course she wasn't pregnant. She was only twenty-three. She was just starting to live life for herself. She had no plans for a baby.

It was just coincidence.

A strange, scary coincidence.

But as the morning wore on Alice became more and more conscious of the way her breasts tingled whenever her arm pressed in as she reached for something. She found herself avoiding the coffee machine as much as possible.

By her break, despite some stern self-talk about not leaping to conclusions, Alice found herself in a pharmacy, handing over hard-earned cash for a pregnancy kit.

It couldn't be. Of *course* it couldn't be.

But it was.

Alice stood in the cramped staff washroom and stared at the indicator that told her she was pregnant.

She didn't slump against the counter. She didn't squeal with excitement or cry. She didn't do anything but stare as the implications worked their way into her brain.

She'd experienced so many life-changing events. Alice had learned railing against fate or trying to avoid reality didn't work.

Her mother had died in a car crash when Alice was twelve. Her father's injuries in the same smash left him in a wheelchair, needing constant support until he'd died of complications when she was seventeen. At least her godfather, David, had given them a roof over their heads when their money dried up and the house had to go. Then David, as close as family, had been diagnosed with a terminal condition. Alice had been the one to look after him through the prolonged illness till last year when—

Alice shook her head. At least, for a change, the latest crisis in her life wasn't about death, but about life. Maybe when she got her head around it she'd even be happy.

She stared into the mirror at the wan-faced young woman whose eyes seemed too big for her face.

Fear stirred.

Fear of the unknown. She knew nothing about babies!

Fear about how she'd support a child when she could barely support herself.

And, yes, a blinding moment of frustration and self-pity. Because, as she'd lost the people she loved, she could find only one positive—that now she could begin experiencing those things her peers took for granted. Parties and carefree weekends. Dating. Starting a career. Going to art school, if she could scrape enough money to support herself.

Now art school would be on hold again, perhaps permanently. She'd have to find a way to support her child, plus a career that earned well and had family-friendly hours.

Alice's mouth twisted at the impossibility of it all.

She grabbed at the counter as another thought struck and her knees gave way.

She'd have to tell *him*. Adoni Petrakis.

For, she realised, she *was* having this baby. She didn't know anything about babies but she was sure she didn't want a termination.

That was one thing sorted at least.

She tried to smile at her reflection and failed. For she cringed at the idea of confronting Adoni. They were from different worlds. It was a miracle they'd ended up in bed together. He was rich, sophisticated and urbane. She was ordinary and embarrassingly inexperienced. More, she'd been downright gauche that night.

The memory always left her torn between horror at what she'd done and a wish that it had never ended. She could get used to a handsome, sexy man with a sense of humour and an appreciative glint in his eyes. A man who was kind and generous and awakened all sorts of unfamiliar desires.

Just as well she'd peeked into his wallet to check his surname. At the time shame had pushed her to spy because in her alcoholic haze she'd forgotten his last name. She'd been determined to know the full name of the man she'd given her virginity to.

Her crooked smile became a rictus grin, her cheeks aching at the pull of taut flesh.

At least she had a name to put on the birth certificate!

CHAPTER FOUR

'MR PETRAKIS?'

'Yes?' Adoni paused on the way into his London office. He smiled at the temporary assistant filling in for his trusted PA, and watched the young woman blush. He repressed a sigh. The sooner his PA returned the better.

'I'm sorry to interrupt.' She glanced to the man beside him. 'But a woman has been ringing quite a lot, wanting an appointment.' Adoni heard what might have been a snicker from Miles Dawlish and the temp blushed even more. 'But her name isn't on the approved list.'

'Then she doesn't get an appointment.' Adoni turned and gestured for Dawlish to precede him into the office. He didn't like the man but the deal he offered was interesting enough to warrant Adoni's personal attention.

'It's just that…' He swung round to find the temp biting her lip. He waited, reining in impatience. She leaned forward, her voice dropping. 'She said it was *personal*. And that it was vital she see you.'

Adoni felt his eyebrows wing up. How difficult was it to get a competent replacement for his sick PA? Surely any assistant worth the name understood the meaning of 'no unapproved meetings'?

The woman's gaze dropped and she fiddled with the notebook on her desk, the picture of guilt. She looked so nervous he almost felt sorry for her.

'What name did she give?' he asked, determined not to scare off another temp.

'Alice Trehearn. She was very insistent. It sounded… important.' The woman looked up, relief in her eyes, but Adoni barely noticed.

Alice Trehearn?

Unbidden, memory unfolded like a bud bursting into bloom. Skin as pale as ivory. A lithe body that responded to him like an instrument tuned to his touch. Lips like crushed berries, sweet and reddened from his kisses.

A mouth that lied. A woman who'd targeted him and played him for a fool.

Yet, even as he opened his mouth to say there'd be no meeting, curiosity rose. What did Alice hope to gain from seeing him? She must have tried his card numbers without success. Was she hoping to seduce him into giving her something else?

The idea of Alice Trehearn trying to seduce him again was undeniably titillating. Especially as Adoni had no intention of letting her get her greedy claws on anything of his. It might be amusing to have sex with her again, purely to finalise unfinished business. Ever since that night a month and a half ago he'd been plagued by the realisation that he still wanted her, despite the fact she was on the make.

Sex with Alice Trehearn still appealed. Almost as much as wiping the smile off her face afterwards when he told her he was awake to her schemes and she'd never get a penny of his.

Adoni smiled at his temp and didn't even mind when the woman blushed and smiled dazedly back.

'Tell her I'll see her. As soon as possible. Here in my office.'

'Oh, but she wondered if you could meet—'

'Here.' Adoni paused, his smile fading. 'Tomorrow. Or not at all.' Then he strode into his office where Miles Dawlish stood. Adoni gestured for him to take a seat.

'I couldn't help but overhear,' the Englishman began. 'I know an Alice Trehearn too. She was at the wedding reception where you and I met. I wondered if it could be the same woman.'

Adoni didn't respond, but took a seat opposite. He had no intention of sharing his personal life. If it weren't for Dawlish's property, Adoni wouldn't waste time with the man. Adoni knew his sort—convinced the world owed him a living. Ready to sell off his inheritance, a truly superb estate, for ready cash.

Even in the days when Adoni had been the favoured elder son of Vassili Petrakis, the billionaire shipping magnate, he'd had to work. He'd learned the ropes in the family company, developing the skills needed to run the enterprise. He'd never have countenanced selling off the family estate.

Those days were long gone. He had no family. His business he'd built by the sweat of his brow. And he wouldn't let anyone, either competitor or thief, take any part of it.

'If it *is* her, the same woman, I mean, you need to be careful.' Dawlish leaned forward. 'Skinny girl, big eyes, smart mouth. Does that ring a bell? She was one of the bridesmaids. Got invited to take part at the last minute. A charitable act by the bride, I understand.'

'I'm afraid I didn't pay much attention to the bridesmaids.' It wasn't a lie. Adoni had barely looked at them, till Alice had pushed her way into his presence and started babbling so artfully about kisses and orgasms. 'But I don't understand. How is an invitation to be bridesmaid charity?'

Dawlish shook his head. 'Not charity precisely. But there was a long-standing rift between the cousins, probably because Alice is such a scheming little…'

'Please. Do go on. I'm fascinated.'

For a moment the other man looked discomfited, as if he realised he'd strayed from the purpose of the meeting. But his hatred of Alice Trehearn needed an outlet. 'Not to put too fine a point on it, she's a conniving bitch.'

'She sounds like a woman to be wary of.'

'Oh, *you'd* see through her in a moment, I'm sure.'

Adoni's answering smile was tight. He'd been furious when he realised Alice had duped him. But learning he was just one of those she'd fooled...

Had he been this incensed when his fiancée Chryssa dumped him and revealed her true colours? It didn't seem possible.

'She tried to deceive you?'

Dawlish shook his head. 'No, I saw her for what she was. It was my uncle she conned. David Bannister.'

'Bannister. The name is familiar.'

'From the documents I sent. He was my uncle by marriage. My aunt, his wife, left the family estate to me but only after David's death. They didn't have children and I was her closest relative. David had free run of the estate while he was alive.' Dawlish clamped his jaw as if grinding his teeth. 'Miss Butter-Wouldn't-Melt-in-Her-Mouth Trehearn moved into his house years ago. She was in her teens, you know, but David was besotted. She could do no wrong in his eyes.'

Adoni frowned. Theft was one thing. But a teenager seducing a much, much older man? Such things happened. Adoni had seen it. Yet it left a nasty taste in the mouth.

'How old was your uncle?'

'In his sixties. Old enough to know better. But they say there's no fool like an old fool, eh?' Dawlish settled back in his seat, stretching out his legs. 'He even let her handle his money, would you believe? And she had the hide to bar my calls and visits, saying David didn't want to see me.'

He sneered. 'But she got her comeuppance. I bet David didn't tell her the estate wasn't his. She probably thought she was sitting on a goldmine and he'd leave it all to her instead of putting it towards running the estate or leaving anything for me to inherit. But she got her hands on everything she could.'

'And was it? Put towards the estate, I mean?'

Dawlish nodded. 'Don't worry on that score. The place is flourishing. David might have been besotted but he'd never let the place go to rack and ruin. He and my aunt even started up an artists' colony a decade or more ago in some of the old estate buildings. You'll see from the material I sent you there are some quite prestigious artists living there. That's in addition to the house and farmlands.'

'It sounds fascinating.' And indeed it was. Adoni and his most trusted staff had been over the details of the place with a fine-tooth comb. It was just what he was looking for. The ancient house would be perfect for a luxury country hotel.

Adoni's fortune was founded on innovative software but he believed in spreading his investments. The upmarket London hotel, another in Santorini and potentially one in the country were part of a plan to ring-fence his wealth.

But of all the things Dawlish told him, Alice Trehearn was most fascinating.

She really was something. She'd almost convinced him he'd taken a virgin to bed, yet she'd been living with a man old enough to be her father, or maybe her grandfather, for years.

Adoni was torn between disgust and curiosity about why she'd show her face again. Did she believe they could take up where they'd left off?

If so, she was in for a short, sharp lesson.

Alice tugged at her cropped black jacket then smoothed unsteady hands down the matching straight skirt as she walked the London street to the address she'd been given. She'd worn this outfit to her father's funeral, then David's. She hated the colour and the memories it evoked, but it seemed the most suitable for today.

It was her going-to-job-interviews outfit. Before David's death she'd worn it again and again while dealing with strangers over estate business. As his illness progressed and he retreated into art and books, David had entrusted her with the day-to-day running of his much-loved property. And while those who lived there knew her capabilities, outsiders saw only her youth and decided she was a pushover to be dismissed or even duped.

Her lips twitched with wry humour. They'd learned. You didn't have to be old to be competent and organised.

Was stark black an improvement on bilious yellow?

Compressing her lips, Alice reminded herself it didn't matter what Adoni Petrakis thought of her appearance. What mattered was delivering her news and discovering if she'd been right about him. She'd been drawn not just to his sexy looks and take-charge air but by the glimmer of humour in his eyes, his tenderness and his patience with a woman who was clearly not at her best.

Surely that boded well? If he were a decent guy, and she had no reason to suspect he wasn't, maybe they could come to an amicable arrangement so their child didn't grow up without knowing its father.

Remarkable how important this tiny baby had become in just a few short days. What would it be like when she held it in her arms? When it was no longer a baby but a toddler, able to run and laugh and hug her back?

A rush of warmth drenched her at the thought of loving and being loved again. This wasn't at all the life she'd planned, but she was determined to look on this pregnancy as a positive, not a burden.

No matter how terrified she was.

Alice swallowed hard, pushing down doubts and fears, reminding herself she was determined and capable. She'd had to be.

What she didn't know she'd learn. And if she was poor—well, that was nothing new. With hard work and maybe some assistance she'd be able to provide for the child.

She reached the glass doors of a sleek building, checked

the address and strode in, not giving herself time to hesitate. Soon after, she arrived at one of the top floors.

The doors opened onto a beautifully appointed reception room. All muted tones, expensive furniture and just a touch of flamboyance in the artful arrangement of exotic orchids and the vast seascape that dominated one charcoal wall.

Maybe it was the art, maybe the quiet air of comfort, but Alice felt the jitters in her stomach ease. She drew her first full breath since she'd begun the five block walk from the underground.

'Ms Trehearn?' A neatly dressed woman approached.

Alice nodded. 'That's me.'

'Won't you take a seat? Mr Petrakis will see you soon. In the meantime would you like tea or coffee?'

'Nothing, thanks.' Nausea had dogged her since she'd got out of bed in the early hours, for the long train trip from the West Country to London. She'd wait till this was over then find somewhere for a nice, refreshing cup of tea.

By the time the receptionist approached again Alice had skimmed four magazines and memorised the painted scene before her.

Had Adoni deliberately kept her waiting? But why? He didn't need to prove a point. She already knew he was powerful and wealthy. She'd done some homework on him. What she'd learned had made it seem as if that evening in his hotel suite was an illusion. What did she have in common with one of Europe's most eligible self-made billionaires?

Sex. That was all.

And now a baby.

The thought calmed the drifts of butterflies in her middle and she smiled at the receptionist's apologies over her long wait.

It didn't matter that Adoni had been heir to one of the world's wealthiest ship owners. Or that he'd been estranged from his family in circumstances no one quite understood. Or that he'd since made his fortune with a software company that grew above market expectations.

Adoni was just a man. Together they'd made a baby. That made them equals in the ways that counted.

If she kept telling herself that she might just get through the next half-hour!

Her first thought on entering his spacious office was that he looked as scrumptious by daylight as he did at night. Though stern, as if he'd just received bad news.

Alice felt a pang of regret. She remembered the conspiratorial smile that had turned his face from sombre and a little haughty to blindingly attractive and beckoningly approachable.

Approachable he was not.

Adoni Petrakis was back to being Ares, god of war. He stood by the window, light slanting across proud, arrogantly handsome features. His thin lips were flat and his nostrils pinched as if against some unpleasant odour.

Alice refused to be intimidated, even though it meant squashing the urge to spin round on her heel and head back out the way she'd come.

This wasn't about her. This was about her child. Their child. She had an obligation to the baby and to Adoni, even if he looked at her as if he'd never seen her before.

Or as if he didn't *want* to see her.

That thought was acid, eating at her composure.

Deliberately she pushed her shoulders back. She'd learned that if she pretended to be strong, even when she was falling apart inside, she could get through most things, one step at a time.

Keep telling yourself that, Alice.

She made herself pace across the room in her freshly polished and only pair of high heels. She ignored the visitor's chair in front of the vast, almost bare desk. She wasn't an employee, here to receive instructions from on high. Instead she skirted the desk and walked right up to him.

Was that surprise flickering in his ocean-bright eyes?

Tucked up in her narrow bed in Devon, she'd told herself she'd embellished his good looks. But, staring up into those remarkable eyes, she realised she'd embellished nothing, except perhaps his friendliness.

'You're not pleased to see me.' She stopped before him, linking her hands to stop them fidgeting under his steady regard.

Had she really hoped he'd be thrilled to have her turn up? All they'd shared was a one-night stand. Not even a night. An evening. A casual sexual encounter.

'I confess I'm intrigued.' His deep voice, at least, was familiar. Too familiar. Heat swept her skin and, in its wake, wave after wave of goose bumps. She'd dreamed of that voice with its suede caress. 'Won't you take a seat?'

'Thank you.' Alice turned, again ignored the straight-backed chair near the desk, and instead crossed to a cluster of lounge chairs. They were grouped beneath an eye-catching work in oils, a wintry city street scene, daring in its use of colour.

The painting eased her nerves. No man with such taste in art could be as ice-cold as he seemed now.

The man she'd made love to—no, had sex with—hadn't been cold at all. He'd been warm and generous and passionate. Where had he gone?

Gratefully she sank into a leather armchair. Stress made her knees wobble and her stomach churn. 'I like your artwork.'

One dark eyebrow rose, a questioning slash on his olive forehead. 'You didn't come here to talk art.'

Alice waited for him to cross and take a seat too, but he remained standing. His cool stare chilled and she fought the impulse to rub her hands up and down her arms.

Okay, he definitely wasn't happy to see her.

Alice pushed aside stupid regret and the even more foolish daydream she'd had that maybe, just maybe, he'd welcome her with open arms, literally. That he'd smile and hold her close and tell her he was pleased to see her. That he'd make everything okay. Even that he'd been searching for her.

She huffed in a little breath of self-disgust. Since when had she believed in such pathetic twaddle?

The answer was easy. Since the man before her, or perhaps his amiable, generous, friendly twin, had seduced her so thoroughly she was more than half in love with someone who existed only in her head. Someone with humour, tenderness, strength and passion.

Alice bit back a sigh and met his guarded stare head-on. 'You're right. I didn't come to discuss art.'

Adoni was stunned at the depth of his response to the slim woman in the sober suit, her dark hair pulled back in an uncompromising arrangement. He had perfect recall of every sinuous centimetre of creamy skin she hid beneath stark black. So perfect he found himself breathing quickly as she sauntered across the room to stare provocatively up at him.

Or was that simply the natural effect of her sulkily sexy mouth and wide eyes beneath long, silky lashes?

No, definitely provocative. Was she annoyed that he'd kept her waiting? He felt his forehead pinch into a frown at the touch of sass he detected in her attitude.

If she'd come to cajole him into an affair so she could part him from his cash she was a little too…deliberate, ignoring the chair before his desk and appraising him so frankly.

He'd expected her to be more conciliatory, more charming. Yet though Adoni felt the impact of her stare like a punch to the ribs, she wasn't conforming to any of the scenarios he'd considered. Neither the vamp nor the tease, nor even the frail female in need of protection.

But then Alice Trehearn hadn't conformed to any stereotypes the first time they'd met either.

Amusement brushed through him as he remembered the outrageous things she'd said that night and her shock as she realised what she'd let slip. Until he recalled it had all been a clever tactic to win his trust and sneak under his guard.

He watched her sashay across to a lounge chair, his gaze roving her tidy, beautifully curved rear as she sank into a seat, her attention apparently on his picture. Beneath the down-lights her hair glowed with a warm hint of auburn.

She was good, he'd give her that. Not even a hint of discomfort on that pale face, though she must know he'd cancelled his credit cards.

Adoni strolled across, drawn despite himself.

Curiosity, that was all.

'You're right. I didn't come to discuss art.' Her voice was husky, as if she wasn't as confident as she appeared. The flickering pulse at the base of her throat drew his eyes and he recalled how he'd kissed her there as she came down from a rapturous high, her whole body quaking. She'd tasted sweet as honey and—

'What did you come for?' His voice was harsh, fuelled by annoyance that the memory of her was indelibly branded on his brain.

She started and her hands clasped tighter in her lap.

'I needed to see you…' She paused and swallowed.

If he didn't know better, he might have been taken in by her sudden show of nerves. She looked paler than before, frail even. But that was an illusion. This woman was tough as tempered steel.

'Yes?' He didn't bother to hide his impatience.

Something flashed in her eyes as she looked up at him. Anger? That surprised him. Surely she was better able to contain her impatience when trying to pull the wool over the eyes of a man she'd targeted?

'You don't want to sit?' No sooner were the words out than she bit the corner of her mouth, as if regretting the question. Because it revealed that he had the upper hand? Or was it some double bluff, designed to make her appear defenceless?

Adoni found his attention lingering on those ripe, dusky pink lips.

Suddenly he lost patience. He'd been curious about her. But now, feeling himself respond to her mixed signals, he'd had enough. He was no one's fool. Not any more.

'No, I don't want to sit. I want you to tell me why you're here. My time is valuable.' Deliberately he crossed his arms.

Something happened to the slate blue of her eyes, as if, just for a moment, they darkened in temper. Then she uncurled herself from the low seat as if electrified.

'Fine. Far be it from me to take up your valuable time.'

She took a step away towards the painting she'd admired, then swung round to face him. Her face looked drawn and that pulse was going crazy, but Alice Trehearn looked anything but vulnerable. She looked defiant.

'The night we had sex.' She seemed to falter and her mouth tightened. 'It had consequences.' Her chest rose and fell as she took a quick breath. 'I've just discovered I'm pregnant.'

Adoni stared at those pretty pink lips, as if, by staring long enough, he could force them to say something else.

Pregnant?

Not likely. He was meticulously careful about protection.

Yet, to his amazement, his belly tightened at the thought of his seed in Alice Trehearn. Of her carrying his child. Some emotion he refused to identify thrummed through him.

Possessiveness?

Absurd. He had no interest in a family. At least not yet. When he did it would be on *his* terms. And not with some grasping thief who saw him as a meal ticket.

The audacity of the woman stunned him. He supposed he should have been ready for this. Instead he'd expected her to try inveigling him into an affair. When she'd arrived, dressed for a business interview rather than a passionate interlude, she'd confounded him.

'Nothing to say? Nothing at all?' That mouth he'd seen tilt down at the corners in a smile he'd found both unique and intriguing turned down again, but not in amusement. She looked indignant as she crossed her arms, plumping up her breasts beneath her dark suit.

'I see.' She bit out the words as if she'd like to take a chunk of his flesh. 'If you think of anything to say about it, anything at all, your secretary has my number.'

She pivoted and strode towards the door, every centimetre vibrating with suppressed energy. It reminded him of the night they'd met, the sensation that she gave off sparks, or that she was likely to detonate with the right trigger.

Oh, she'd detonated all right.

Adoni reached her in two strides, his hand curling round her upper arm, drawing her inexorably back towards him.

'Not so fast, Ms Trehearn.'

CHAPTER FIVE

HIS VOICE WAS a snarl and his big hand was brutally hard.

And, to her absolute horror, Alice felt, muddled in with her indignation, a tremor of excitement at finally getting a reaction from Mr Superior.

No, no, no.

She was not going to let him get to her.

Or play those man-woman games she was sure to lose.

She was a novice and Adoni Petrakis was too adept.

Alice drew herself up as tall as she could, doing her best to ignore her body's mixed signals—jaw clenched in anger, knees shaky with something close to fear and, worst of all, that snaking coil of sexual response drawing her belly tight.

Though she hated his aggressive attitude, Alice's body responded as if expecting more of that sensual bliss he'd bestowed. As if he'd imprinted himself on her psyche and she associated him with amazing sex and the euphoric sense of well-being that had stunned her when he'd held her close.

The thought appalled.

Deliberately she looked at his big hand on her arm, then up into that beautiful dark face with its infuriatingly condescending expression.

'There's no need to get physical, *Mr* Petrakis. I'm happy to stay and discuss this now you've found your voice at last.'

Was he grinding his teeth? A muscle jumped in his jaw and her chin hiked higher. *She* had nothing to apologise for. He'd been in a bad mood since the moment she'd arrived.

With a slight shake of his head he released her. 'Sit down, Alice. We need to sort this out.' He turned his back and strode to the desk, murmuring something into the phone, presumably to his secretary.

Alice sank back into an armchair, surprised at how shaky she felt. She hadn't expected this to be easy but nor had she expected outright animosity.

'You say you're pregnant?' Adoni lowered himself into a chair opposite, his long legs stretched out as if he hadn't a care in the world. Yet his face looked as hard as if it was cast in bronze.

'I *am* pregnant. I saw a doctor yesterday.'

'And you'd have me believe the baby is mine?'

Alice bit back the instinctive retort that rose to her tongue, ignoring the flicker of hurt that he'd think she'd lie about something so fundamental.

He didn't know her, after all. Just as it was becoming clearer by the moment that she didn't know him either. She'd thought him…nice, caring and tender, funny and—

'Having second thoughts about your story, are you?' He leaned forward, his scrutiny so keen Alice swore she felt it scrape over her features like a blade.

'It's no *story*. I wouldn't be here if it wasn't true.'

His eyes narrowed to gleaming slits. 'How convenient that none of your other lovers, before or after me, was so… potent. Incredibly potent, since I took the precaution of using a condom.'

It took enormous willpower not to respond to the snarky innuendo in his tone. Alice refused to lower herself to his level. 'Condoms aren't foolproof, as any medical practitioner will confirm. And as for other lovers…' She paused, feeling heat rise in her cheeks.

'You were saying?' Adoni steepled his hands under his chin as if weighing every word.

Damn. Alice hadn't wanted to admit this, but it seemed she had no choice. 'There haven't been other lovers. Either before or after.' Sheer willpower kept her staring into his narrowed eyes, despite the embarrassment curdling her insides.

Adoni's expression didn't alter, other than a slight puckering of his forehead.

The silence thickened and Alice felt a horrible sensation creeping up her spine to tighten the back of her neck, as if gnarled fingers fastened round her nape.

'You expect me to believe you were a *virgin*?'

Alice tore her gaze away, down to her knuckles, clenched in her lap. 'I know it's probably unusual these days, but yes. I was.'

When she looked up Adoni had tilted his head to one side as if to view her better. 'And what about your long-term lover? Or doesn't he count?'

'Long-term lover? I don't have a lover.'

He leaned forward, teeth bared in what might have passed for a smile if it didn't make Alice think of a ravening wolf. Even his teeth were white and almost perfectly straight!

'That's not what I hear. In fact I'm informed you're a *femme fatale*, living off gullible men.'

Alice shook her head, bemused. 'You've got me confused with someone else.'

'No. *You've* got *me* confused with someone who'd fall for your lies.'

'I'm not lying! I never had a lover before…you.'

Where had all this animosity come from? She'd shared things with Adoni Petrakis that she'd never shared with anyone. She wouldn't have known him for the same man who'd laughed with her and made love so wonderfully.

'Really? What about David Bannister? I hear you lived with him for years.'

'David?' She frowned, sitting back in her seat. 'How did you…?' Alice shook her head. It didn't matter how he knew, just that he'd misunderstood. 'You've got it wrong. David was a friend.'

'A very dear friend. Much older and very wealthy.' Cynicism dripped from every syllable.

'That had nothing to do with—'

'It seems to be a habit of yours, making *friends* with older, wealthy men. Like when you barged into my private space.' He leaned nearer, his gaze needle-sharp. 'Did someone tell you that night that I owned the hotel? Or had you been planning your approach for some time?'

'No!' Alice threw up one hand, trying to stem the flow of accusations. 'You've got it all wrong. I'm not like that.' Her breath came in short, hard gasps. If it weren't so appallingly horrible, it would have been absurd. Her, as a gold-digger! 'Whoever told you about David made a mistake.'

Adoni's lip curled. 'Which is what I'd expect you to say.'

The feral light in his eyes, the cruel twist of his mouth and the furious rasp of that deep-pitched voice cut through Alice's composure. Suddenly she felt not indignant but anxious. It was clear mere words wouldn't convince him.

Once, maybe, she'd have stood her ground and made him eat his words. But she'd changed. Maybe it was exhaustion from her first ever bout of full-blown morning sickness on the train this morning. Or the primal need to remove her unborn child from the vicinity of danger. But suddenly she was on her feet, putting the chair between her and the man giving off such waves of aggression.

The door opened and his secretary came in, carrying a tray with cups and a cafetière. The woman slanted a surprised look at Alice, then placed the tray on a low table, said something to her boss and left.

Alice pried her fingers off the back of the chair and turned to follow her, feeling as if every move took far too much effort. Stress, she assured herself.

She'd only taken a few steps when the scent of coffee hit her. Good strong, aromatic coffee. The sort she'd once loved.

Bile rose in her throat and she gagged. She froze, one

hand going to her stomach and the other to her mouth. Time splintered as she fought against the indignity of vomiting here, in front of this inimical stranger.

Then Adoni was standing before her, those winged eyebrows scrunched in concern. 'What is it? You look grey.'

'Coffee,' she whispered. 'The smell.'

For a second he stood, uncomprehending, then he whipped round, grabbed the tray and carried it out.

When he got back Alice had found his private bathroom. Her hands were braced on the edge of the black marble basin and she was shaking. She hadn't been ill this time but it had been a close call. Nausea still hovered and her mouth tasted of acid.

Studiously she avoided her image in the mirror. Instead she took slow breaths, willing the nausea to subside.

'Alice?' His voice was deep and soft. If she closed her eyes she could almost believe herself back in his luxury hotel suite when he'd been charming and gentle.

She sucked in a hiss of air then croaked, 'I'll be okay in a minute.'

Silence extended, then she heard running water. A moment later damp towelling settled on the nape of her neck, cool and surprisingly refreshing. Without hesitation she let her head droop forward, accepting his ministrations.

After a couple of minutes he murmured, 'Turn,' and it seemed natural to comply. Still with eyes shut, she leant back against the basin while the damp cloth traced her cheeks and mouth, her forehead and throat.

Alice swallowed, surprised to find herself reviving now the pungent aroma of coffee was gone.

'Sip this.'

She opened her eyes, locking onto his serious greeny-blue stare. Something shuddered inside. Not fear or indignation but something vital that even nausea hadn't dimmed.

She looked down to the glass of water he held to her

mouth and took it from him, careful not to touch his hand. Obediently she took a tiny sip, then another, relief settling around her shoulders as her stomach didn't revolt.

'Thank you.'

He surveyed her, unblinking, from under hooded lids. Dully, Alice wondered what he saw, or thought he saw. She'd be distressed by his distrust when the nausea passed. Right now she didn't have the strength to be anything other than grateful for this ceasefire in his antagonism.

'Can you walk?'

She nodded, stifling the urge to ask whether he'd carry her if she couldn't. It was crazy the way she craved his tenderness. His solicitude changed nothing. He thought her a liar.

Alice took a deep breath and looked towards the door to the office. It seemed a mile away. But she hated appearing weak, especially to someone with such a low opinion of her.

Setting her jaw, she took a careful step forward. The room pitched then settled. She took another step. Only a few score more to get out of here.

Except Adoni moved, swooping down to tuck an arm beneath her knees and wrap another around her back. He held her high against his chest, her head against his shoulder as he carried her into his office.

'This is unnecessary,' she whispered, her throat raspy. 'My legs work fine. It's just morning sickness.'

Adoni didn't answer. Instead he settled on a long sofa with her on his lap. Water spilled from her glass onto her skirt with the movement but she said nothing. It felt so good to be held against his powerful body. That intense heat of solid muscle was soothing and he was surprisingly comfortable to a woman who felt as powerful as a blossom in a strong wind.

If she rested just a moment to regroup she'd be ready to go another round or three with him.

'Try one of these.' His voice rumbled up from some-where below her ear as he leaned forward, reaching for the coffee table. The movement folded her closer into his body so she was enveloped by him, breathing in the elusive scent of cedar and spice that had entranced her that night in his bed. Her nose wrinkled. Strange how this scent didn't seem to disrupt her upset stomach.

He cradled a small bowl of pistachios.

'I don't want to eat anything.'

'It might help. When my stepmother had morning sick-ness she used to nibble salted wafers and nuts.'

Alice looked down at the broad, bronzed hand cupping a silver bowl. Surprise burrowed through her at the inti-macy of that revelation. Tentatively she took a nut, its shell half open.

'Bite gently on the shell and it will open completely.'

Alice complied, relishing the salty dusting on the out-side and the soft nuttiness inside. She slipped the shell into her hand and swallowed the pistachio.

Hesitant, she waited, but her stomach didn't heave.

'Try another.' Adoni proffered the bowl again.

'Thanks, I will. But I'd rather sit alone.'

It was a lie. Alice had never felt more comfortable than slumped, half-boneless, against Adoni's strong form. Which was unbelievable, given his earlier animosity.

After the shock and anxiety of this week his powerful masculinity propping her up felt ridiculously reassuring. Except that was a temporary illusion. He didn't trust her. Worse, he despised her. And even if he didn't she couldn't afford to get accustomed to the idea of anyone else looking out for her. The news of her pregnancy had reinforced the fact that she had no one to rely on. It would be up to her to look after herself and her child.

He stiffened. Then, without a word, he lifted her and put her down on the seat beside him.

Fleetingly Alice thought about how much upper body strength it took to manage that. Till her brain kicked into gear, reminding her she had other things to concern her than Adoni Petrakis's muscles.

'Eat.'

She nodded and tried another pistachio, sucking the salt from the shell, then methodically chewing the nut. She'd never had pistachios before. 'Are these Greek?'

'They are,' he murmured.

'I like them.' Strange how easily the words came. Almost as easily as that first night. The memory of her unguarded, downright outrageous behaviour drenched her in sudden heat and she pushed the bowl away.

'You feel sick again?' His voice came from near her ear as if he leaned closer. Alice wondered at the concern in his voice.

'No. I'm okay.' She took another sip of water and shut her eyes, willing herself to concentrate. It was difficult to whip up indignation against the man who'd just tended to her so carefully. She didn't know where she was with him.

Finally she leaned forward and put her glass down on the coffee table with a decisive click. Then she swivelled to face him.

Troubled eyes met his. Adoni couldn't see any hint of the woman he'd expected, the woman who'd set him up to bleed him dry. Yet looks deceived.

He felt a pang of regret. He was torn between that and ingrained caution. There was no doubt that physically Alice Trehearn was weak. Feeling the tremors running through her slim frame and seeing her distress at almost being sick evoked long-dormant instincts to protect. He'd gathered her to him and almost *wanted* to believe in her. Just as he'd been drawn to her the night of the wedding, charmed by what seemed a uniquely refreshing woman.

Yet there was nothing unique about a woman scamming a rich man.

'You still don't believe the baby is yours.' Her voice was flat but her eyes pleaded for understanding. Did she really think his unwilling sympathy over her nausea would blind him to the bigger picture?

'No, I don't.' He ignored the flare of apparent hurt in her eyes. He knew how well a woman on the make could pretend.

'So where does that leave us?'

'Simple.' His voice was harsh. Yet to his amazement what should have been simple—getting to the bottom of Alice Trehearn's allegation—was mired in unexpected emotion. 'Have a paternity test. If the child is mine, then we'll talk.'

Her eyes darkened and she looked away, but not before he read hurt there. Again, Adoni found himself torn. His silent applause at her dramatic skills warred with a sliver of guilt that perhaps he had this wrong and she was, against the odds, an innocent.

'Of course.' She seemed to gather herself. 'I'll be in contact when it's arranged.' Then she shifted to the edge of the seat and made to rise.

Adoni's hand shot out, grasping her arm, holding her where she was.

'What?' Her dark gaze met his before sliding away.

'Where are you going?' Surely she wasn't well enough to leave? She still looked parchment-white. Besides, she hadn't yet broached the all-important issue of money.

'Home. If I leave now I can be back in Devon in time for my evening shift.'

'Evening shift?' Even now she trembled beneath his hand and the fragility of her slim body struck him. Surely she wasn't well enough for work?

'I'm a waitress.' She looked pointedly at his hand on her sleeve, as if waiting for him to remove it.

'A waitress who can't stand the smell of coffee?'

Her lips tugged into a crooked smile for just a second before she saw him watching and pursed that lovely mouth. 'Ridiculous, isn't it? But hopefully it won't last long. Now, if you'll let me go I'll be on my way.'

With deliberate slowness Adoni released his hold and sat back, crossing his arms. The gesture masked his reluctance to release her. It had been like that the night they'd met—that urge to touch, to caress, to connect.

'Surely not,' he drawled, watching her like a hawk. 'Didn't you come here for money?'

Her head whipped round, hectic spots of pink colouring her cheeks. She drew herself high, perching on the very edge of the sofa, and surveyed him down the length of her not very impressive nose.

'No. I came here because I felt you deserved to know you're going to be a father.'

'So getting rid of the child didn't occur to you? You're definitely having it?'

She nodded and Adoni felt the old distrust spike. Of course she'd have the child if she thought there was benefit in it.

'Ah, but would you have made the same decision if I weren't rich?'

Instantly the pink drained from her cheeks and her skin took on the greenish pallor she'd worn when she battled nausea.

'That's a foul thing to say.' Her eyes looked huge and wounded.

Adoni met her stare unblinking. 'It's a cruel world. There are plenty of women who'd barter a rich man's child for an easy life, or dispose of an inconvenient one.'

Her nostrils flared and her mouth tightened. 'I'm not one of them. And if that's the only sort of women you know, I pity you.'

'It's not pity I need. Just the truth.' His jaw clenched and his chest rose as he dragged in a calming breath.

How dare she take that attitude with him? Just because he faced facts. It was true, the women who'd figured largest in his life had been devious and disloyal, but he was the last person to need pity. Especially from this slip of a girl.

'So tell me, *Alice*.' He leaned close, pinioning her with his eyes, daring her to lie barefaced. 'Didn't you come hoping I'd give you money?'

She blinked, her gaze dropping for a tell-tale moment. Strangely, Adoni didn't feel triumphant but disappointed.

Slowly she nodded. 'Well, yes. I thought you'd probably want to know our child and build a relationship with her or him. And I hoped...' She swallowed and stared straight back at him. 'I thought you might contribute later. You know, for school costs and that sort of thing.'

'Not now?' His lips curled derisively.

'Now?' Fine vertical lines appeared on her forehead. 'It hasn't even been born.'

It was Adoni's turn to be surprised. Was she for real?

'Surely there are expenses?' He let the words hang. Given the chance, she'd no doubt fill it with a wish list of comforts.

She shook her head. 'Not so far.' She paused. 'I was going to buy some pregnancy books but the local library had some excellent ones.'

When he remained silent she continued. 'One of the other waitresses has a pram and cot and other bits and pieces in good condition. She swears three boys are enough and she won't have more children, so she'll let me have what I need.' Alice's hint of a smile died as she registered his expression. 'What? What's wrong?'

What's wrong? Either Alice was the most convincing actress he'd ever met or his baby was going to grow up in the wilds of Devon, surrounded by second-hand furniture and reliant on the goodwill of others.

There are worse ways to grow up.

What did luxury and money matter when there was no honesty, much less genuine love from those closest to you?

'Adoni?'

Get a grip, man. You don't even know if it's your child.

'Nothing is wrong. I was just thinking.'

Since when had he been unable to think and speak at the same time? Adoni found himself reacting viscerally to this situation, instead of logically. Betrayal by a woman he'd trusted, however fleetingly, cut too close to the bone.

For a decade he'd guarded his heart. Hell, he probably didn't have a heart to guard. He liked women physically, but he allowed none close emotionally. Casual and mutually pleasing was how he kept his relationships. He'd learned distrust in a hard school and would have bet his fortune that no woman would ever unsettle him again.

Alice Trehearn did it with just a look.

Yet, unaccountably, he discovered within himself an unexpected yearning for the very thing life had taught him he couldn't have—an honest, caring woman. A family.

Adoni hated to acknowledge it, but the prospect of fatherhood ignited a firestorm of emotions and memories. Of blissful happiness, trauma and finally abandonment.

Alice eyed him doubtfully. 'So, I'll ask my doctor about a paternity test and—'

'No. I'll arrange it. You'll be contacted.' Adoni had no intention of taking the word of someone Alice lined up to advise on the baby.

She nodded and got to her feet.

Adoni repressed the urge to bar her way. She was pale and he registered smudges of tiredness beneath her fine eyes that he hadn't noticed before. But she didn't need him to care for her, even if that was what she was ultimately angling for.

He rose, noting how her chin reflexively notched higher as if she was determined not to let down her guard around him. That made two of them.

'My PA has your contact details?'

Alice nodded, then paused as if waiting for something. A kiss? An offer of lunch? Or something more? The stormy light in her eyes told him something was going on in that pretty head of hers. It infuriated him that he couldn't interpret her expression.

'Goodbye, Adoni.' Without waiting for a response, she turned and walked straight-backed out of the room.

Adoni noted the finality of her tone. Because he'd called her bluff and he'd never see her again?

He wished it were that simple but, in his experience, life rarely was.

CHAPTER SIX

ALICE SMILED AT the elderly couple. 'Of course it's okay to change your order.' Again. 'I'll just nip into the kitchen and sort that out.' But she'd have to be quick.

Turning, she threaded her way between the tables, pushing exhausted muscles to hurry, though it felt as if she were wading through treacle, her feet ridiculously heavy. She glanced at her watch. Another hour. Could she make it to the end of her shift?

She'd been grateful for the additional work when one of the other girls hadn't been able to come in, knowing it meant a little extra in the bank for when the baby came. Yet now she felt worn too thin. Exhausted as she was, she couldn't sleep properly.

Was she doing the right thing, severing contact with Adoni? Not taking the paternity test he'd demanded?

It was a major step, one she couldn't take lightly. Yet the things he'd said in London, his ultra-cynical attitude… She wasn't sure she wanted him helping bring up their child.

Not that he would. His idea of involvement was probably throwing money at the kid. Paid nursemaids and posh boarding schools, rather than love and caring.

He'd made it clear he had no interest in the baby, other than as a financial burden or a tool for blackmail. She shivered, wondering what sort of world he inhabited where distrust and deceit were the natural order.

Wearily she pushed open the door to the kitchen and relayed the change of order. Then she grabbed a glass of water and slumped against the wall. She needed to catch her breath long enough to get through the next hour.

Alice closed her eyes, taking another slow drink. Had

she done right, telling Adoni's PA when she'd rung to arrange the paternity test that she'd changed her mind? She wasn't going through with the test.

He'd think it was because the child wasn't his.

The trouble was, this way she'd deny her baby the chance to know its father. If she had the test, Adoni would be involved in their baby's upbringing. Yet Alice feared what that meant for the child.

And for her. Because even while he'd been spouting the most abhorrent accusations, she'd found herself craving the physical comfort she remembered from Adoni's embrace. When she was nauseous and, instead of walking away, he'd cared for her, she'd felt almost ready to forgive him his doubts.

How dangerous was that?

She refused to become a woman who made excuses for a man's bad behaviour. Who knew where that would end?

'Alice, there you are.' It was Viv, her boss. 'Hey, are you okay?'

Alice straightened and opened her eyes. 'Just grabbing some water. I'm running on empty today, but don't worry, I'll go and—'

Viv waved her hand. 'That's what I came to talk to you about. You look done in. I've called Chrissie and she's coming straight over. She'll be here in five so you can grab your stuff and go.'

Alice stared. She couldn't help it. Viv was a decent boss, but she'd never before noticed when Alice felt on the verge of collapse, which had been several times lately. Even when the morning sickness was at its height, fortunately only for a short time, Viv had been almost oblivious, concentrating on her booming business.

'Go on, what are you waiting for?' Viv smiled. 'I'd be hurrying if I had such a good-looking escort to take me home.'

'Escort? I don't have an escort.'

Viv's blonde eyebrows rose and her smile was positively girlish as she nudged Alice. 'Keeping him quiet, are you? That's fine, love, so long as no one else sees him. But even in that tucked-away corner he's attracting a lot of attention. If I were you I'd get my skates on.'

'But—'

'No buts.' Viv pushed her towards the cupboard that served as a locker for staff belongings. 'You don't keep a man like that waiting.' The older woman gave a slow wink. 'Especially since he persuaded your boss to let you leave early. Now, get going before he comes in here to see what's taking so long. He looks the sort to do just that.'

To Alice's astonishment she heard a rasp of approval in Viv's husky voice. Viv who, as far as she knew, cared for nothing but her café and her two cats.

Dazed, Alice relinquished her order pad, put on her jacket and shoulder bag and walked back into the café.

Instantly her gaze turned to the far side of the room from the tables she'd been serving, to the dark corner couples often chose for its intimacy.

Her eyes bulged. Her breath was a sharp indrawn hiss.

She almost backed into the kitchen, thinking of the rear exit into a deserted lane.

But it was too late. Adoni Petrakis had seen her.

He got to his feet, apparently oblivious to the stares of every woman in the room. His gaze was fixed unerringly on Alice. She felt it like the stroke of one large hand sliding across her cheek, down her throat and settling like a warm weight around her.

His face was impassive, utterly unreadable, yet her heart thrummed impossibly fast as she met that penetrating stare.

He wore a crisp white shirt, golden cufflinks at his wrists. His black hair gleamed in its perfect cut. Against the rich olive skin, his eyes were bright as the Mediterranean on a hot summer day. Or maybe that was Alice, her temperature rising as he prowled towards her with the lithe, concentrated grace of a natural predator.

She swallowed and backed a step, only to find her heels rapping the kitchen door. Another staff member was trying to come out and Alice stumbled forward.

Hard hands caught her. Hands that felt appallingly familiar. Her dreams were peppered with vignettes of those hands, and that amazing body, doing the most wondrous things to her.

'Alice.' His low voice was a wash of heat across her skin. 'We need to talk.'

'Not here.' She was conscious of the curious stares, not only from customers. The back of her neck prickled and she guessed the other staff were craning for a view of the Greek god who'd descended into their midst. He looked as out of place amongst the farmhouse chic and cream teas as a lynx in a litter of tabby cats.

'No, not here.'

Two minutes later they were on the narrow pavement and his hand was still on her elbow as he led her towards a classic vintage sports car.

Alice stopped short, her sensible shoes gripping the cobblestones. 'No. I don't want to go in your car.'

He arched one jet eyebrow, his face impassive. 'You'd rather have our discussion here?'

Other pedestrians brushed past, hurrying as the damp, fog-laden air pressed down on them. From the corner of her eye she saw faces in the bow windows of the café turned towards them. Adoni Petrakis was the biggest thing to hit town in a century or two. No doubt everyone was wondering what he was doing with someone as ordinary as Alice.

'There's no need for a discussion. We can agree to go our separate ways.' Even as she said it, Alice knew it wouldn't work. Adoni looked as immovable as the tors on Dartmoor.

He didn't bother to reply, merely raised that other winged brow in silent query.

Alice shivered and pulled her thin jacket tight round her. The weather had changed for the worse since she'd arrived this morning, taking her by surprise. Which showed how distracted she was. Normally she was far more organised.

Alice suspected the chill she felt owed little to the gloomy weather and more to nerves.

Adoni moved abruptly, swinging his jacket around her shoulders, enveloping her in cashmere warmth and a tantalising aroma of cedar wood and male skin. She shivered again and this time she feared it was with sheer sensual delight.

'You look exhausted. I'll take you home.' Then he was opening the car door and ushering her in and Alice found any inclination to object had fled. Was she so easily seduced by the promise of physical comfort? Or, worse, by this man who viewed her as a gold-digger?

Maybe exhaustion had overcome caution.

She should have realised she couldn't just walk away from him. He'd want absolute certainty the child wasn't his. Even though he clearly didn't want a child, Adoni Petrakis was too definite, too emphatic to leave anything to chance, especially the possibility he'd fathered a baby.

He got into the car, filling the space with his long body and her senses with his presence. The air seemed to crackle with an excess of energy and the fine hairs on her body stood to attention. Alice bit her lip and looked out of the window as he switched on the ignition and pulled the purring vehicle out onto the street.

Faces slid by, hurrying pedestrians. She heard the swish of tyres on rain-slicked streets and watched the buildings pass till finally, as they drew up to the kerb, her mind processed what had happened.

'You know where I live?'

He said nothing, just switched off the engine and got out. Alice was still fumbling with her seat belt when her door opened and he leaned in, unfastening the buckle. Her fingers were all thumbs.

'How do you know where I live?'

She should have waited till he stepped back to ask. Instead he leaned into the car, his face mere inches from hers, those polished eyes so close she could make out the rays of green mixed with the blue. It was like staring at some exotic sea and feeling the undertow drag her down. Beautiful but dangerous.

'I know much more about you than that, Alice.'

She watched his mouth form her name, heard the faint, delicious foreignness of it on his tongue, and felt something shudder to life deep inside. She moistened her lips with her tongue and was surprised at the flare of interest she read in his eyes.

How could that be? He thought her a lying tart. He couldn't be attracted to her.

And she should be completely indifferent. He'd insulted her in the worst possible way. Pride dictated that she feel nothing but contempt for him.

Yet it wasn't contempt trailing lazily through her body. The realisation scared her.

'What do you mean, you know more about me?' Realisation struck and with it her laggard indignation. 'You had me investigated?' Her voice rose to a ragged screech. Suddenly the close confines of the car were too claustrophobic. She put her hand to his shoulder and pushed.

Finally he withdrew and Alice stumbled out onto the pavement.

'You had me investigated.' She couldn't quite believe it. It sounded like something in a movie.

Alice shivered at the thought of paid investigators digging into her past, maybe interviewing friends and acquaintances, prying into her personal affairs. Not that there was anything to hide, but the idea made her feel grimy.

Apparently this too was the norm in his world for he shrugged those straight shoulders and spread his hands.

'Why not? Surely I have a right to know about the woman who claims to be carrying my baby.' His voice rang out in the quiet street and Alice found herself looking around, but they were alone.

Adoni had no such qualms about being overheard. 'Before that all I knew for sure was that you can't hold your liquor and that you have an interesting chat-up line.' His eyebrows lifted in that superior way of his. 'About orgasms, as I remember.'

Heat scorched her cheeks and she squirmed inside. His face was solemn as a judge but she knew he was smirking at her. 'That wasn't a chat-up line.' He made her sound like a cross between a lush and a vamp.

Or maybe just a fool for ever thinking she had anything in common with Adoni Petrakis.

'If you say so.' That casual shrug was supremely annoying, as if it didn't really matter what she thought or said.

Alice grabbed the luxuriously warm jacket engulfing her and shoved it against his chest. He was the most infuriating man she'd met. Right up there with David's nephew, Miles Dawlish. How come the only nice guys were a generation older than her?

'Thank you for the lift.' The words shot out. 'But I'm feeling unwell. I need to rest. If there's anything else, I suggest we sort it out over the phone.'

It wasn't gracious of her. She sounded downright waspish, but he deserved it. Besides, it wouldn't do him any harm to learn the world didn't dance to his tune.

Without waiting for goodbyes, Alice swung away, grabbing the key from her bag as she stalked up the cracked path to her ground-floor bedsit. Through the front door, then her own door and—

A large form crowded her from behind as she tugged the key from the lock.

'Hey, I—'

'Allow me.' Adoni's hand covered hers. Before she knew it he had her key and her door had firmly shut behind him.

Alice opened her mouth to blast his impudence, but—

'Here. You need to sit.' Quick, deft hands undid her jacket and tugged it from her shoulders as he pushed her into the room's one ancient armchair. 'A cup of tea? That's what you English have as a restorative.'

Without waiting for a response he was investigating the couple of white-painted cupboards in her tiny kitchen corner, pulling out a mug and a canister of tea bags.

'Leave it. I can do that.' Alice levered herself up, vaguely surprised at how heavy her arms and legs felt after that marathon shift. But then Adoni loomed over her again.

His brows pinched down. 'Stop fussing. I'm not going to steal the family silver, I promise.' He paused and she watched, fascinated, as he drew in a deep breath that hefted that impressive chest high, almost as if he found this situation as difficult as she did.

'I'm not leaving till we've had our chat, Alice, so you might as well make yourself comfortable and rest up. You look like hell.'

CHAPTER SEVEN

IT WAS A LIE. She looked weary but her dark blue eyes glittered bright as jewels and the spots of blush pink on her cheeks emphasised the delicacy of her features and her pale, fine-grained skin. The indignant jut of her chin drew attention to that memorable mouth, and as for her supple body...

Adoni was stunned by the wave of hunger that swept him, remembering how good they'd been together.

But he was here for answers, nothing more.

'You might as well sit, Alice. I'm not going anywhere.'

'Give me my key.' Her jaw tilted higher.

Slowly Adoni withdrew it from his pocket. He took her hand and raised it, palm up. She was trembling, ever so slightly. Sensation sparked where they touched and an answering resonance, low down in his belly, heralded the reawakening of that desire he'd never quite banished when he was with her.

He pressed the metal into her palm and closed her fingers over it, his eyes locked with hers, reading her confusion and turmoil. It was as if she didn't understand or couldn't accept the quick, hard pull of attraction between them. As if it frightened her.

He'd almost feel sorry for her, except he still wasn't sure about her. She could be as honest as she appeared or a talented liar. He resented the games she played. First that surprise announcement of a pregnancy, then a complete withdrawal.

Why?

Second thoughts about trying to con him?

A miscarriage?

Adoni's mouth settled into a grim fold at the sharp slicing sensation through his middle.

The kettle boiled and he swung round. 'Milk? Sugar?'

'Milk, please.'

He opened the tiny fridge, taking time to peruse the contents. Milk, butter, two eggs. A pot of yoghurt. And on the tiny kitchen counter a bowl with a couple of pieces of fruit. She was eating sensibly but there didn't seem to be much of anything.

Adoni frowned. The whole place, what little there was of it, was sparse. The bed pushed up against the wall was a single, the table was tiny and the wardrobe meagre. The only signs of bounty in the place were the bookshelves bulging with paperbacks and a collection of exquisitely executed botanical studies on one wall.

He opened another cupboard. Rice and dry pasta. A tin of fish. Plain cracker biscuits.

'What are you looking for? I don't take sugar.'

He swung round, his eyes roving her slender form. Had she lost weight since he'd seen her? Shouldn't she be putting on weight?

He took two paces across to her chair and passed her the mug. She took it slowly, careful not to let her fingers brush his.

Adoni found himself staring at the milky paleness of her flesh so close to his deep olive skin. That night in his bed her pink and white softness against his bronzed flesh had added to the potent eroticism of the experience. Just looking at her had wildly aroused him.

Even now...

Then he noted how she cradled the hot drink in both hands as if she were cold.

'Have you seen a doctor?'

'I told you, I saw one to confirm the pregnancy.'

'I mean since then. You've lost weight.'

She shrugged and took a tiny sip of tea, her shoulders easing down a fraction. 'The joys of morning sickness. I'm sure I'll put on weight soon enough now that seems to be passing.'

It was on the tip of Adoni's tongue to question further, till he caught himself. He needed to get back to the main agenda.

'You agreed to a paternity test. Why change your mind? If you're scared of the risk to the baby, I'm informed there's a newer non-invasive test that doesn't affect the child at all.'

She looked down at her tea, avoiding his eyes. Was that guilt he read?

Abruptly her head lifted. 'First, answer a question for me. If it *were* your child, what would you expect?'

'Expect?' Adoni frowned.

'Would you expect to be involved in his or her life? Or would you...' she waved one hand '...just offer some financial support and stay out of the picture?'

Was she serious?

The idea of his child growing up without him sent a shudder of revulsion through Adoni. The very idea tapped into the vein of unresolved emotions that eddied like a dark, poisonous current within him.

He felt his blood thicken, his pulse grow heavy, as anger simmered. 'No child of mine will grow up unacknowledged.'

He barely recognised the voice as his own. Before him Alice blinked hard and sat further back in her chair, looking at him as if she'd never seen him before.

'Every child deserves to know its parents.' Adoni paused, swallowing the bitter taste of outrage.

His child—if it *was* his child—would be not only acknowledged but loved, and accepted always.

'When I have children I will be an intrinsic part of their

lives.' Anything else was unacceptable. 'Now, answer *my* question. Why change your mind about the paternity test?'

Here was her chance to admit the child wasn't his.

Strange he didn't feel more relieved at the prospect.

After reading the short dossier on her, he'd almost come to accept that the pregnancy had been a result of their evening together. According to the investigator, Alice Trehearn had spent the last six months living here very quietly. No reports of men in her life at all.

As for the couple of years she'd lived with David Bannister in his historic property near Dartmoor, there'd been very little detail on those. The locals, when questioned, had been surprisingly unwilling to gossip about the young woman who'd shacked up with a wealthy man so many years her senior. But this baby couldn't be Bannister's. Alice was still in the early phase of pregnancy and Bannister had died too long ago.

Eyes as dark and bleak as the evening sky met Adoni's. 'I didn't follow through because once you had confirmation the baby was yours there'd be no going back.'

'Sorry?' He folded his arms over his chest. She was talking in riddles.

She pursed her lips and turned away, staring out of that small, bare window. 'I went to see you in London because I believed a man should know if he's going to be a father. But after the things you said, the accusations you made...' She shook her head and wisps of rich, glossy hair framed her face. 'I don't want my child to grow up in a world where cynicism and money are more important than trust and love. I don't want my baby growing up tainted by that.'

She turned back, her eyes locking on his, and Adoni read, not calculation as he'd expected, or even nerves, but disdain.

Alice Trehearn had judged him and found him wanting? Preposterous!

Of course he'd been doubtful. Only a fool would take such a statement at face value, especially given his history. Adoni was no fool. He'd learned his life lessons. Caution, hard work, reliance on self rather than others, distrust of emotions and of the motives of beautiful women. All had served him well. He saw no reason to change now.

It was outrageous that she'd judge him on his initial response to her news. She couldn't seriously demur at his involvement with the child.

Adoni's brain circled her words. 'You mean it really *is* mine?'

Slowly—reluctantly, if he was any judge—she nodded.

Instantly sensation exploded in his belly. Not desire. Not anger. Excitement. Tiny ripples of it rayed out like aftershocks from an earthquake. Adoni sank onto the hard little bed opposite her, hands knotted on his thighs.

Her word was no proof. But teamed with the investigator's report…

He leaned forward and she shrank back, clutching the mug. 'You were going to let me believe the child was someone else's? Is that why you withdrew from the paternity test?' His voice bit like bullets, shattering the silence. 'Because you, in your infinite wisdom, decided I wasn't fit to be a father?'

The nerve of the woman!

Adoni had thought he'd known anger. He *had* known it. He'd dredged the depths of fury and despair in his time.

But nothing prepared him for the surge of adrenaline that pumped through his blood, hearing she'd considered having his child in secret. Or perhaps not having it at all!

To be deprived of his own flesh and blood?

He who had no family at all?

Adoni shot to his feet, paced to the window then spun to march back to the door.

Damn this tiny room. There wasn't space to breathe, much less think.

He turned and strode to the window, planting his fists on the sill and watching rain stream down the glass.

'I don't honestly know.' Her voice was muted as if it came from far away. Perhaps the thunderous pulse in his ears blocked his hearing. 'I needed time to think. What you said, the way you were in London, scared me.'

Adoni swung round, stunned. 'I would *never* hurt a woman. Or a child.'

Yet there was a brittle quality about Alice as she watched him that told him she wasn't ready to trust.

Adoni scraped a hand across his collarbone, rubbing hard. The situation was laughable. It hadn't been confirmed that the child was his. Yet there she sat staring down her nose at him as if he were the one who didn't measure up.

A maelstrom of emotions warred inside him.

Adoni, with his usual single-mindedness, ignored them. Emotions didn't help. They made you weak and you had to be strong to survive in this world.

First, he had to establish if the child was his.

Second, if it *was* his, he and Alice needed to discuss the future. There would be arrangements to make, legalities to finalise.

He glanced around the sad little bedsit. Not here. His brain wouldn't even let him picture his child here.

He breathed deep, considering his options.

If the paternity test confirmed her statement, there was one obvious path that would ensure the child's future.

Marriage. It would cement his absolute right to bring up the child as he saw fit.

Except his distaste for marriage was all but insuperable, given Chryssa's betrayal and that of his mother. Just the thought of it made his skin crawl. To be tied to a woman he barely knew, when those he'd thought he'd known absolutely had betrayed him utterly?

No, that wasn't the answer. Which meant any other arrangement they made had to be completely watertight.

As the child's mother, Alice could be an ally or a formidable opponent, with rights under the law that couldn't be ignored. It was imperative they forge an understanding. Imperative she trust him.

Instead of looking at him as if he were the Prince of Darkness himself.

Adoni forced himself to take a seat on the narrow bed, composing his features. 'I'll have my PA reschedule the paternity test for tomorrow.'

Slowly, she nodded. 'If that's what it takes to convince you.'

He told himself things would be so much simpler if the baby were someone else's. Yet already he was working on the basis Alice carried his child. His gaze dropped to her flat belly. Instantly she stiffened.

How different she was from the uninhibited, passionate woman he'd met in London. That inner fire and her cheeky attitude had attracted him. Along with that sexy, streamlined body and a mouth so delectable it made his head spin just looking at it.

Adoni spread his hands in a posture of openness. 'In the circumstances my reaction to your news was reasonable.' Alice opened her mouth but he lifted a hand, stopping her. 'I can understand why you thought it wasn't, but our experiences have been different. I know you had a close-knit family.'

'I have nothing to hide. Anything you wanted to know you could just have asked, instead of paying an investigator to pry.'

At least now she looked haughty rather than spooked.

Adoni preferred that. Alice's spirit had appealed from the start.

'Only a very little prying,' he murmured. 'I know you were born in Cornwall, only child to artistic parents, and that apparently you were all very happy together.' Until her mother died in a car crash that put her father into a wheelchair.

Adoni was tempted to probe about what came more recently, her years as David Bannister's live-in mistress. But that wasn't the point. The point was this child and securing the future Adoni wanted for it.

'You didn't have a happy childhood?' Her expression softened though she still looked wary.

'It was okay, with a workaholic father and a mother whose passion was shopping rather than family.' He shrugged. 'After she died my father married again and my stepmother was pleasant enough.'

Alice frowned. Clearly she deemed 'pleasant enough' unsatisfactory. Which was a good thing, he decided. If he was seeing the real Alice, then surely it meant she'd aim to do far better for their child.

Their child. The idea, so outlandish still, unnerved him. He, Adoni Petrakis, a father!

His actions now would set the tone for their relationship and, most importantly, his child's future.

It was time to win Alice's trust, even if it meant breaching the barricades of his reserve. For trust didn't come easily to him any more. Not since he was nineteen.

Not even Chryssa, his ex-fiancée, knew the reason he'd been disinherited. But after years of reticence Adoni no longer cared who knew this particular truth. It was no reflection on the man he was. The only one whose pride would be punctured if the revelation became public was Vassili Petrakis.

Adoni's lips curved. It would be almost fitting if Alice

Trehearn took the story to the media. But he doubted she would. He was beginning to suspect she wasn't the woman on the make he'd accused her of being.

He wanted to believe in her. That, in itself, rang warning bells. For there was no empirical evidence he was wrong about her. Why would Dawlish tell outright lies about her? Adoni didn't like the man but that didn't negate his claims. Besides, Adoni had learned enough to know extreme wealth attracted clever, unscrupulous women.

'Tell me then.' Alice put down her mug and folded her arms across her chest, presumably unaware of the way it plumped her breasts against her shirt. 'What do you think excuses your attitude to me in your office? Or, for that matter, your arrogance in having me investigated?'

Instead of being annoyed by her questions, Adoni nodded, as if acknowledging her right to ask. The hard stare, guaranteed to shrivel impertinence, had disappeared. Yet Alice was sure she read tension in the set of his jaw and the fast tic of his pulse at the base of that strong, bronzed throat.

'How about the fact that's exactly what my mother did?'

Alice frowned. 'Sorry? I don't understand.'

He leaned back on hands splayed wide on her bed. He looked far too at home on the thin mattress. Alice was distracted by the realisation she'd be haunted by the memory of him there when she tried to sleep later.

He'd stalked into her home and completely filled it with his presence. Even the air smelled different, spiced with an exotic tang that lingered in the nostrils, teasing with the hint of warm male skin and testosterone.

Adoni shrugged, the movement dragging her attention to those powerful shoulders then back to that lean, sculpted face. 'My mother got pregnant. She then went to a very rich man, the sort of man who could provide for her and her baby multiple times over, and seduced him, persuaded him the baby was his. He married her and brought up the baby, believing it was his.'

Alice felt her mouth sag in astonishment. She didn't know what she'd expected but it wasn't this. It sounded so callous, so ruthless. So scheming.

That was why he'd accused her of being a *femme fatale* who lived off men? Because his own mother—?

'For years no one knew the truth. Till one day the old man had a hospital procedure. In the process he discovered from his blood type that his eldest son couldn't possibly be his son.'

Alice's eyes felt round as saucers. Adoni was talking about himself, not a sibling. She knew from her recent research that he was the eldest son in the family, his younger half-siblings being around a decade younger.

She tried and failed to imagine what it would be like, having that bombshell dropped on you. To discover everything you knew about yourself and your family was a lie.

'Your mother? Did she explain?'

Adoni shook his head. 'We only discovered the truth when I was nineteen. My mother was dead by then and no, she never told me the truth. So, you see, all we know for sure is Vassili Petrakis *isn't* my father. She lied to us both and took my real father's identity to the grave. I have no idea whose bastard I am. It's too late to revisit history and try to discover who she slept with.'

Adoni's thin lips stretched up in a smile that looked as affable as a hangman's noose. 'In the circumstances, I think it quite reasonable I'm wary of a woman I barely know telling me I'm about to become a father.'

Alice's breath was an indrawn hiss. Of course he was wary. Her revelation must have seemed like history repeating itself or, judging from his eyes, like blows to an unhealed bruise. For, despite the adamantine strength of his jaw and the assured tilt of his head, Alice saw a flash of something else in his expression. Something akin to pain. It was gone in a second and she'd never have noticed it except she'd seen its echo in the mirror from time to time when her resilience cracked and grief welled.

Looking at Adoni now, she read only assurance. No hint of distress.

'I'm so sorry,' she whispered. 'I don't know what to say.'

He shrugged. 'Nothing. It was all a long time ago.'

'But to do that to you, and your father...' She shook her head. 'It must have been...'

'It's water under the bridge.' Adoni slashed the air with a dismissive gesture. 'At the time I thought it vital I discover who fathered and abandoned me. But I realised it was a waste of energy. My identity isn't about my parents. It's about what I make of my life. Who I've become.'

He paused, and Alice saw he was watching her absorb his words. Yet he wasn't looking for sympathy. The stern set of his lips and the arrogant tilt of his head reminded her he was no longer the bereft teenager he must once have been. This was a powerful man in control of his life and his world.

Until you sashayed in and told him he was going to be a father.

Was that why he'd been so furious? Because this was something he had no control over?

Or was it that the situation cut too close to the bone? Because it required him to overcome his prejudice and trust her.

'I'm not like your mother, Adoni. I didn't plan this.' Surely he realised that? He'd seduced *her.*

He regarded her without comment and Alice felt a little twist of distress as she realised that, given his history, he couldn't possibly take her word for that. He couldn't trust her.

'I'll take the paternity test tomorrow.'

He nodded, abruptly. '*Efharisto.* Thank you.'

Adoni took one of her hands in his. His were large and capable. There was a dusting of silky black hair across his olive skin and Alice had sudden, intimate recall of his naked body, the same lovely burnished colour all over. Heat bloomed and she swallowed hard.

'I may have reacted badly, Alice, but don't judge me on that.' Absently he stroked her thumb. 'Just as I won't judge you on the fact you got drunk and put the hard word on a total stranger.'

She stiffened, yanking her hand back, but he merely tightened his grip. 'I didn't—'

'Shh. That doesn't matter.' This time he stroked his thumb across her palm and she shuddered. To her horror she realised it wasn't indignation rippling through her, but arousal. 'What matters is the baby.'

'Exactly. The baby.' Alice nodded, her head moving jerkily as if pulled by a string. It was difficult concentrating on his words when her body responded so flagrantly.

Her *pregnant* body. Surely sexual arousal should dim with pregnancy, shouldn't it? She knew so little about this stuff!

Looking into those mesmerising eyes, feeling the evocative tug of his deep voice right at her very core, Alice didn't *feel* pregnant. She felt hot and bothered, tense and aware and…interested.

'There's no need to worry, Alice.' Did he misread her distraction? She was just giving thanks that he'd misconstrued her reaction for nerves when he continued.

'If the child is mine I'll be there every step of the way.' His gaze dropped to her abdomen in a provocative, assessing stare.

Just as before, Alice felt a shudder of elemental response tear through her. It started as embarrassment but that was eclipsed by a jagged gouge of physical arousal and a bone-deep thrill of power.

Because there was something like possessiveness in his unwavering gaze and warm grasp. As if, despite himself, he too approved and wanted. Not just the baby, but *her*.

Pride, logic and modern morals told her she should require far more from a man than *want*. But in her state of heightened awareness, Alice had never known anything as powerful as the urge to reach out and test the boundaries in the most primitive way possible. To push a little and rediscover the heady sense of oneness she'd discovered with Adoni, the sheer carnal pleasure of melding with his beautiful body.

He leaned closer, his fresh breath soft on her cheeks. 'If this child is my flesh and blood, my *only* flesh and blood, I'd never abandon it. I'll do whatever it takes to keep and care for it. To guide and protect it. I'll be part of its life every day.'

Alice met his unwavering gaze as his words penetrated. Abruptly that swell of arousal faded.

By admitting the baby was his she'd removed the safety net she'd craved—time to consider whether she really wanted Adoni Petrakis and his sophisticated, cynical world to impinge on her baby's life, and hers.

The dynamic between them had shifted irrevocably.

Adoni had money, prestige and authority. He was her baby's father and, it was now clear, he had every intention of being a hands-on father.

How far would he go to ensure that?

She knew nothing about the legalities. She told herself firmly that there was no way he could have the baby taken from her so he got sole custody. Was there?

Another tremor racked her, yet this time it wasn't the heated rush of excitement but the chill cascade of fear.

CHAPTER EIGHT

'THE CHILD IS MINE? You're absolutely sure?' Adoni planted a hand on the gleaming desktop, the phone clamped to his ear.

'Yes. It's yours.' The voice kept talking about DNA and percentages but Adoni didn't take the words in. 'Yes' was all he needed.

His heart hit an unfamiliar rhythm. Quick and—could it be—triumphant?

It didn't seem possible. His life was meticulously planned. An unexpected child hadn't been in his schedule.

That changed now. Everything changed now.

He'd thought he'd prepared himself for the possibility that Alice carried his child. But nothing could have prepared him for the deeply visceral response welling in his taut body.

His child.

His flesh and blood.

His family.

The words thrummed with each pulse of blood in his arteries. They carved themselves into his bones and shuddered through his cramped lungs.

'Thank you—' he cut across the speaker '—and yes, I want the report in writing.'

Adoni hung up and stared across his office at the view of central London, the sky a mix of pale blue and grey cloud that still felt alien, even after years using this country as his base.

Suddenly, unaccountably, he found himself longing for the endless bright skies of his childhood summers in Greece. The scent of wild herbs crushed underfoot, the salt tang of the sea, sharp and beckoning as he clambered down the track to the coast. The freedom to run wild whenever they left Athens for their country estate.

Abruptly Adoni shoved his chair back and strode to the window.

Was that what he wanted for this baby?

He had a country retreat there, in the final stages of completion. But it was a retreat, not a permanent home. His business was in the city.

Yet even as he thought it, Adoni acknowledged he could run his business from wherever he wanted.

What came first was his child—what was best for it. One thing was certain. His child wouldn't live in a dismal bedsit. It would have the best of care, as of now.

His baby would be protected and nurtured. Loved as Adoni had never been, with his mother intent on pleasure and his supposed father engrossed in money-making.

Adoni picked up his phone.

'Greece? You can't be serious!'

'It's an excellent idea.'

Alice digested the cool certainty in Adoni's voice and stifled a bubble of hysteria.

Her? Go to Greece?

She took a slow breath, then another. She stood hunched in the overhang of a shop roof, sheltering from the persistent rain that had already soaked the bottom of her trousers as she walked to work.

She'd got a passport years ago but never had a chance to use it. Never gone further than London.

An image she'd once seen filled her mind. Brightly coloured boats bobbing in the crystal waters of a sun-drenched harbour. In the foreground, under the shade of a spreading tree, were tables and rush-bottomed chairs of vibrant blue. The elegant townhouses crammed around the cove were a wash of pastel colours that invited you to forget your cares and drink in the scene.

A cold, fat drop of rain hit her cheek and slithered down her neck. Alice rubbed her chilled flesh.

'I can't drop everything and go to Greece. I have a job and—'

'That's no problem.'

The soft burr of Adoni's deep voice made her shiver, but not from cold. She didn't even like him, did she? Yet she responded to him every time. As if they shared some secret link, some affinity. 'Sorry? I missed that.'

'I spoke to your employer.'

'You did *what*?' Her voice rose and a woman bustling down the narrow pavement gave her a wide berth.

'I explained you needed rest to regain your strength—'

'You told her I was pregnant?' Alice's temper soared. Usually she was slow to anger, her emotions under control.

Adoni Petrakis, however, had a knack for igniting her fuse.

'Of course not. I just mentioned I was concerned for your health.'

'That isn't something you should discuss with my boss.' Severely, Alice repressed the idea of a holiday. It was a luxury she couldn't afford. 'If I want to ask for leave *I'll* do it. But I can't. I haven't been there long enough and it's busy—'

'But you can.'

'Pardon?' Alice drew her collar closer and scowled into the rain that had graduated from a miserable drizzle to solid sheets of icy water.

'She is happy for you to go.'

Alice frowned. It sounded unlikely. They were rushed off their feet. One waitress was off with a broken leg and another on compassionate leave to care for her sick mother.

'I can't leave my job.' Because chances were there'd be no job to return to.

'Are you always this obstinate?'

'Are you always such a bulldozer?'

His laugh, a rich, baritone chuckle, was like liquid chocolate, warming her chilled bones. 'Touché.' He paused. 'If it's the income you're thinking of, I'll cover your expenses while you're away. And your rent.'

Was the man a mind-reader?

Yet it wasn't just the money; it was the way he'd dealt direct with Viv, interfering outrageously now he was sure Alice carried his child.

She tried to whip up fury but instead sagged back against the wall of the shop.

Adoni was right. The long hours she was working, taking extra shifts in the scramble to save as much as she could, were getting too much.

Nor could she really blame him for needing proof of paternity. They were strangers. Despite the quickening she felt whenever he came close, or like now, when his treacle rich voice was soft in her ear.

'Think of the baby,' he purred. 'It needs you to be healthy and well-rested.'

'Lots of women work during pregnancy.' If he tried to make her feel guilty...

'Of course, but I'm sure most would appreciate some extra rest. Besides, we have decisions to make for the future. Wouldn't you rather do that when you're refreshed and on vacation?'

Alice's nerves twitched at the determination she heard on the word *decisions*. As if he had very definite views on their child's future and intended to have his say.

I'll be there every step of the way.

I'll be part of its life every day.

'I can't talk now. I'm late.' She lifted her head and more windblown drops spattered her cheeks.

'We *do* need to talk. To work out the details.'

It was on the tip of her tongue to say they'd got this far without working out any details. But he was right. She just wished she didn't feel so hemmed in, by him and the pregnancy.

'I'll call you later, Adoni.'

But switching off her phone didn't banish his words. Especially when she arrived at the café to find Viv talking about *when* she went to Greece with that delectable man. How *nice* he'd been. How *considerate*. He'd even arranged an interview with someone from his London hotel who wanted to relocate to the country. Viv was excited about the new waitress with her experience in a top London hotel but adamant there'd be a job for Alice on her return.

Then Alice's landlord confirmed that next month's rent had already been paid.

In the end Alice found, to her chagrin, she had no excuses left.

She was going to Greece with the father of her unborn child. The only man who'd tempted her into letting go and living for the moment. The one man who still tempted her in ways she refused to think about.

Typically, Alice refused to make things easy for him. Any other woman would leap at the idea of lounging in luxury by the Aegean. Not Alice.

Because she was determined to prove she wasn't a gold-digger? Or because she genuinely had other priorities? What could they be?

Adoni set his jaw as he left the elegant Georgian mansion he'd just inspected and followed a path through the woods that he'd been assured led to a cluster of estate houses.

He'd planned to be in Greece by now. Instead he was in

rural England, collecting Alice from an engagement she'd insisted she couldn't miss. She'd promised to catch the train to London when it was over, but Adoni had no intention of kicking his heels at the airport, perhaps receiving a message that she'd been delayed.

He'd rearranged his schedule to take another look at the property he planned to purchase. The very property where Alice had lived with David Bannister. The property Bannister's nephew, Miles Dawlish, had approached Adoni about buying.

The manor house was perfect for the exclusive country hotel retreat Adoni envisaged. As for Dawlish's plans to get the adjoining swathe of land rezoned for housing, that didn't bother Adoni. The manor would be secure in its landscaped valley, surrounded by woods on three sides and the moor behind it. Besides, his contacts advised the rezoning application was doomed to fail.

Dawlish had done Adoni a favour, bringing the place to his attention. The man was greedy, his asking price inflated; he was desperate for a quick sale to cover escalating gambling debts. The sale would proceed on Adoni's terms, not Dawlish's. The sting in the tale was that, while the sale would make Dawlish solvent again, the man would have to change his lifestyle and work for a living if he wanted to keep his head above water.

As for Dawlish's warning about Alice being a conniving slut—

Adoni frowned. Had Dawlish feared she'd seduce David Bannister into leaving more of his personal funds to her? That she'd somehow break the inheritance? Had that tainted his view of her?

Yet Alice had openly lived here, with a man old enough to be her father, supported by him. Adoni had prowled the vast, elegant house with the agent, assuring himself it would suit his purposes. Yet all the time he'd thought of

Alice there with her much older lover. Seen them sprawled across the vast four-poster bed in the master suite. Envisaged Alice, her moonlight-pale skin bare as she stretched over the shining ebony of the grand piano in one of the salons, her ripe mouth curled in an inviting smile.

His pace quickened as he passed a dappled glade of bluebells, their sweet scent at odds with the acid in his throat.

She'd lied about her sexual experience. She must have. She'd been thoroughly debauched by the time she reached Adoni's bed.

Debauched? He sounded like someone from another century, full of double standards. He didn't give a damn how many men she'd been with. All that mattered was securing the child she carried. *His* child.

His thoughts were an unsatisfactory whirl of conjecture when he stepped out of the woods and discovered a cluster of picturesque cottages. They lined a narrow lane, half of them thatched and white-washed and the other half stone-built and equally attractive with quaint windows and roses around the doors.

Adoni had expected a ramshackle collection, ready for the bulldozers that would clear the farmland beyond if Dawlish's plans proceeded. Instead, they appeared in excellent condition.

Laughter drew his attention, husky and low-pitched. The skin at his nape pinched in anticipation.

Alice. His belly tightened and so did his groin at the memory of that throaty laugh in his bed that memorable night. Of the caress of her sweet breath on his bare skin and the taste of her luscious mouth.

Adoni quickened his step and saw her outside a cottage with two men, one grey-haired and smiling down at her. The other, with an unkempt shock of white hair, had his arm around her shoulders.

Something dark and chill engulfed Adoni.

Maybe she was genuinely attracted to old men. The idea made Adoni grimace.

Or perhaps they were simply easier to dupe, eager for a pretty young woman's company.

He strode closer and the trio turned.

'Adoni.' Alice sounded breathless and her chest rose quickly as if in agitation. In her short-sleeved floral dress she looked fresh, young and innocent. Then her smile solidified. Adoni took in her flushed cheeks and the glitter of her eyes and thought he'd never seen her look lovelier.

The knowledge didn't improve his mood.

The shaggy-haired man at her side narrowed his eyes under tangled white eyebrows. 'I hear you're taking Alice to Greece.' His deep voice boomed like the sea thundering into a cave. 'I expect you to look after her.'

'Jasper!' She turned, breaking his hold and frowning.

'I am and I will.' Adoni held his gaze. 'She'll be better off with me than working herself to exhaustion.'

The older man stared a moment longer, then nodded abruptly. 'That's what she said.' He turned to Alice. 'But don't forget, there's always a place for you here. Maureen and I have missed you.'

Alice's smile this time was wide and genuine. 'Maybe Maureen has, though how you'd fit another person in your cottage I'm not sure. And I know you, Jasper. You've probably been so busy in the studio you don't even know what month it is.'

She turned to Adoni. 'Let me introduce you. Adoni, this is Jasper Hyde, an old friend of my family, and—' she gestured to the other man, silent beside them '—Felix Christow, down from London for the day. Felix, Jasper, this is Adoni Petrakis.'

Adoni shook hands, amused by Hyde's punishing grip, as if he sought to deter Adoni with a show of strength.

'A family friend?' Adoni queried.

'Yes.' It was Alice who answered. 'My father and I moved into the end cottage after...' she paused '...when I was twelve. Jasper and Maureen were our neighbours. They looked after us.'

'No more than you did for us, Missy, these last years when David got sick.'

'David?' The name shot out. Were they talking of her ex-lover?

'David Bannister,' Jasper said. 'Our friend and land-lord. He lived in the big house I hear you're planning to buy. He created the artists' colony here with his wife, years ago. A good man.' He shook his head. 'Unlike his obnoxious nephew.'

The third member of their party spoke up. 'Well, it's time I headed back to London. Thank you for your help, Alice, Jasper.' He shook hands with each in turn. 'I'll send invitations to the opening.'

'I'll look forward to it.' Did Adoni imagine it or did Alice's eyes glow more brightly?

'Nice to meet you, Mr Petrakis. Perhaps I'll see you at the opening too.'

As his car drew away Adoni turned to Alice. 'Opening?'

'Felix is curating an art exhibition in London of my mother's work.' She sounded proud and excited. 'I promised to meet him to provide some background information for the exhibition.'

Jasper Hyde scowled. 'He doesn't even know? Yet you're haring off to Greece with him?' The old man's disapproval showed in his mottled features.

Alice shrugged, obviously uncomfortable. 'It's not like that. We're not...'

Jasper raised abundant white eyebrows and Adoni was fascinated to see colour wash Alice's cheeks. He had no idea what was going on, but if he didn't know better he'd believe Alice was nervous about telling the old man exactly what linked them. Sex and an unborn baby.

A strange attitude for a woman who'd openly lived with her previous lover on this estate.

'It's time we left,' Alice said quickly. 'It's a long way to London. Give Maureen a hug for me and—'

'Don't forget that jam she made. I'll never hear the end of it if you go without it.'

Alice nodded and, with one wary look at Adoni, hurried towards the back of the cottage.

She was barely out of sight when the other man spoke. 'I expect to see Alice come home looking much less peaky.' He swivelled and Adoni was surprised at the force of his piercing gaze. 'You haven't done a good job looking after her so far, for all your money.' His gaze skated over Adoni's tailored clothes with disapproval. 'She's not entirely friendless. If you hurt her—'

Adoni lifted his hand, palm outward. 'I have no intention of hurting her.' He was torn between annoyance at the man's presumption and curiosity that Alice had such a vehement champion. 'If I'd had my way she'd have been on vacation a week ago.'

'Ah,' Jasper said. 'She always could dig her heels in. Just as well, or she'd never have been able to manage this place.'

Adoni frowned. 'Manage *this* place? The estate?'

The old man nodded. 'Ridiculous, isn't it? People thought David mad to hand over the reins to a slip of a girl. But she was a quick learner and she knew the place like the back of her hand. She loves it. Unlike that bumptious nephew of David's. He'd run it into the ground.'

'You're telling me Alice Trehearn managed this whole estate?' It wasn't possible, surely. In addition to the manor house, which was in pristine condition, there were farms and woodlands, this cluster of cottages, all by the look of them in fine order, and—

'She did.' The old man's smile faded. 'Not that I approve of what David did, mind you. Say what you will, it was selfish of him burdening her. But who could blame him?'

Adoni was torn between curiosity and a deep reluctance to hear details of her life with her sugar daddy.

'Here we are.' Alice appeared, brandishing a jar of jam, surveying them speculatively.

Adoni's mind raced. Was she a gold-digger with a talent for good management? Jasper Hyde didn't seem the sort to be seduced by a pretty face yet he was protective of Alice. Clearly too she'd left the estate in good condition, though her own financial circumstances were dismal.

Was her poverty real, or a ploy for sympathy?

Not having answers drove Adoni crazy.

He stirred from his reverie as Alice kissed Jasper on the cheek, promising to send photos of Greece. Jasper growled something about being careful, then Alice and Adoni turned back to the path through the woods.

'What were you and Jasper talking about?' Her voice was high, almost breathless.

'You.' Adoni saw her start.

'What about me?'

He was tempted to string her along, sure he'd discover more about her if she was on edge. But he preferred the truth. 'About you running the estate. Why didn't you mention it?' His investigators had neglected to add that, though they had referred to her having access to Bannister's accounts. Adoni had taken that as proof of her avaricious ways.

'Why should I? It's not relevant.'

Adoni disagreed. Anything about her character was relevant while he tried to determine who the mother of his child was.

Especially when he responded to her more than was desirable. Like now as she marched beside him, her narrow jaw set and a frown knotting her brow. They passed through the perfumed dell and Adoni wanted to pull her close, discover if her hair still smelled of orange blossom and if her skin was as satiny as he recalled. If she'd sigh a welcome as he took her voluptuous mouth. How would she respond if he powered her down into the swathe of bluebells and—?

'You let me think you were just David Bannister's lover.'

Instantly her full lips pinched and her nostrils flared in distaste. 'I did no such thing! *You* came to that conclusion.' She paused, her breathing fast and shallow. 'I don't need to explain my past. Besides, you wouldn't believe the truth if it rose up and bit you.'

Adoni looked into bruised blue eyes and felt his chest constrict. 'You could try me.'

'Could I, indeed? That wasn't what you said in London.' Her hands jammed onto her hips and her chin tilted. 'Besides, you've set yourself up as some sort of judge! It's none of your business.'

She whirled round, her skirt belling around shapely legs, and stalked down the path.

Adoni watched her go, grumpy yet tantalisingly sensual as she strode away. Dappled sunlight picked out the dark auburn in her hair and the natural sway of her hips ignited a pulse of unwilling, inevitable awareness.

She was the mother of his unborn child.

Adoni was stuck with her. He needed to know her, understand her. For his own sake.

Because he wanted her still. Again.

And he intended to have her, on his terms.

But he refused to be duped again.

CHAPTER NINE

'WHAT ARE THOSE THINGS?' Alice peered from the helicopter at the square towers rising from the tiny village below.

She'd got over her initial nerves about flying in the machine soon after they left Athens. Now she was storing impressions of the country she'd only seen on film. She'd expected Greece to be all white beaches and endless blue skies, but there was much more.

Adoni turned, his eyes locking on hers, making her skin tingle. 'Houses.'

'Houses? They don't look like it.' They were like windmills without the sails, or watchtowers.

An expression she couldn't decipher played around his mouth. 'Welcome to the Mani. It's a peninsula at the southern end of mainland Greece. We do things differently here.' The pilot said something in Greek and Adoni laughed.

'Why do they have towers?'

'Because the locals are known for holding grudges. In the old days their feuds sometimes lasted years. They were renowned as proud fighters. Each tower—' he waved a hand '—was once the secure part of the house. The windows are small so defenders could shoot at their neighbours.'

Alice shivered. 'It sounds grim.'

He smiled. 'We don't generally shoot these days.'

'You're from here?' Alice gazed at the barren mountains whose folds plunged into the sea. Some seemed almost bare and others were carved into narrow terraces. It looked wild and windswept yet majestic. Here and there more fertile areas showed green.

They passed another village, a cluster of stone houses and square towers.

'Yes, I'm a Maniot. I was born in Athens but my…father's family is from here.' Alice heard repressed emotion on the word *father* and winced inwardly, remembering what Adoni had said about his parents. He didn't know who his biological father was. 'This is where we came for feast days and holidays. It's where I've built my own retreat.'

As if on cue the helicopter swooped low. Ahead was a cove, its waters aquamarine. A cluster of buildings sheltered at its centre and small boats floated on the crystal sea. On the far side was a headland with a tumble of houses and a now familiar tower.

But it was the building on the nearest headland that caught her breath. Built of local stone, it resembled a traditional tower. But there the resemblance ended. This tower had windows so large she saw right through to the other side. And below it on ground level sprawled a stone and glass building that extended to hang suspended over the steep slope to the sea. The result was unique, daring but elegant, yet part of the landscape.

'That's your house?' Alice turned to Adoni as the chopper came in to land. She hadn't expected this. His grand London hotel and David's estate in Devon that he was negotiating to buy were both traditional.

'It is.' His eyes met hers but she had no idea what was going through his mind.

'It's…amazing. Truly original.'

Those winged eyebrows soared. 'I'm glad you like it. I didn't know you had an interest in architecture.' Was that approval in his expression? Warmth?

Alice's breath thickened, her skin tingling as it too often did around Adoni. Even when she thought she might hate him for his high-handed ways and his determination to think the worst of her, she couldn't quite kick that fillip of excitement when she got close to him. When he looked at her like *that*.

Deliberately Alice turned to watch as the pilot landed on the helipad behind the house.

'There's a lot we don't know about one another.'

Those words proved truer than she'd realised.

First there was the welcoming committee. Not just employees, though there'd been some of those and Alice noted that Adoni treated them like everyone else—with a smile. There were also neighbours who came up from the village to welcome him.

'This is the first time I've visited since the house was finished,' he told her. 'They're curious to see it.'

But it was more than curiosity Alice read in their smiles. It was genuine welcome.

Adoni had urged her to go and rest, saying there was no need for her to stay if she was tired, but she wouldn't have missed the impromptu party for anything.

It wasn't how she'd pictured a billionaire's housewarming.

There was no couture fashion though Adoni, in snugly tailored black trousers and a green shirt that almost matched his eyes, looked like a model for an upmarket magazine.

There were no socialites, but, judging by the callused hands she shook again and again, people who worked hard. There were old folk in dark colours, their faces weathered, and younger ones who were happy to practise English. Children raced across the terrace, laughing, making Alice smile.

She'd been nervous coming here, worrying that she handed Adoni too much power, being in his territory for the discussion about the baby. But as the afternoon drew into evening Alice felt more relaxed than she had in months.

Home cooking scented the air as people arrived with

platters and a spit roast was set up. Instruments appeared and music, unfamiliar yet enticing, began in competition with the babble of people having a good time.

'How are you bearing up?' That dark voice feathered her ear as long fingers gripped her elbow. Instantly her insides did that funny roll and flip as sensation shot from Adoni's touch to the apex of her thighs.

Alice frowned at the fruit juice in her hand. She couldn't even blame alcohol for that response.

Throughout the evening Adoni had kept checking on her. She'd look up to find his eyes on her. Inevitably her thoughts would tangle and she'd lose track of the conversation.

'What's wrong?' Concern tinged his voice. 'Are you feeling ill?'

Alice made herself meet his gaze. There it was again, that whump of sensation when she got too close to Adoni.

It was hard, staring up into that solicitous expression, remembering that he thought her a *femme fatale* who preyed on men.

She swallowed a bubble of laughter. Anything further from the truth she couldn't imagine.

'I can rest later. I'm enjoying myself. Everyone is so friendly.'

He shrugged. 'It's a small community.'

But it wasn't just that. Alice had already heard from several people how Adoni had helped out when a fishing boat had been destroyed in a winter storm. How he'd found work for someone else. How he'd ensured there was a better medical service for the area.

Adoni Petrakis, international tycoon and bane of her life, was respected and liked.

'You're popular,' she murmured and was surprised at how easily she accepted it. Despite the atrocious way he'd behaved when she'd told him about the pregnancy, despite his take-control attitude, Alice grew convinced that Adoni Petrakis was a decent guy, most of the time.

Those wide shoulders lifted. 'They know me. I've been coming here since I was born.'

'The locals back home know Miles Dawlish but they don't welcome him like this.'

As soon as the words slipped out Alice knew she'd said the wrong thing. Adoni's forehead scrunched up in a furrow of displeasure. He dropped her arm as if stung. Alice was sure he'd got the outrageous story about her being David's lover from Miles. The guy was poison and he judged by his own standards. Miles couldn't believe she hadn't been interested in David's money, grabbing what she could for herself. Clearly, he believed any friendship between a man and a woman must be based on sex. He knew nothing of respect, caring or obligation.

The reminder was a sluice of icy water down Alice's back.

'You're wanted.' She nodded to a man approaching from a cleared space on the wide terrace. He said something in Greek, a grin splitting his face. Around them clapping started in time with the music.

Adoni turned, paused briefly, then with a nod left her. He joined the older man at the centre of the terrace. Another joined them, then another.

'You like dancing?' It was a woman she'd spoken with earlier.

'I don't know. I've never really tried.' There hadn't even been a dance at the wedding, since her groomsman partner had been too drunk. Before that she'd been too busy for dances.

'Really? We'll fix that, later. But first watch. You'll enjoy.'

And she did. The music, slow at first, had a rhythm that caught the blood. It was the perfect vehicle for the men to show off. For that was what the dance seemed all about. They formed a line, moving slowly in time with the tune.

At their head the leader, sometimes Adoni, sometimes another, would leap, drop and spin with a measured grace and a rampant athleticism that was all the more impressive for being carefully controlled.

Alice found her gaze following Adoni even when he wasn't in the lead. Watching the rhythmic sway of his body, the proud, upright posture, the deliberate, steady movement of his feet. She recalled his talk of the tough, warlike people who'd carved a life for themselves out of this beautiful, harsh environment.

Swallowing hard, she followed the twist and dip of his broad, straight shoulders, the arrogant angle of his jaw, the strength and potent masculinity in those long legs with their muscled thighs.

As if sensing her regard, Adoni turned, eyes locking with hers.

Something passed between them, as quick and devastating as an earthquake. It rumbled up from the soles of her feet, through her belly where, amazingly, their baby lay cradled, to her chest. It interfered with the beat of her heart, making it quicken and jolt.

Still Adoni held her gaze. From this distance, in the failing light, his eyes looked like dark velvet. Her attention dropped to his mouth and the tremor intensified.

He felt it too. She could tell. It was there in the cut glass angle of his cheekbone where the skin pulled too tight. In the jut of his jaw and the flare of his nostrils.

The heat eddying in Alice's belly flared into a conflagration that roared and swirled, blotting out the music, singeing her nerve endings.

'Excuse me,' she murmured to the woman beside her and swung away.

Adoni farewelled the last of his neighbours. One final pat on the back, a promise to catch up over a game of *tavli* and a glass of ouzo, and he stood in the moonlight, watching the stragglers head down the road.

He was glad of the dim light, for their welcome had moved him. He hadn't lived here for years, though he'd been back often lately, keeping an eye on building progress. Yet the whole community had come out to welcome him.

It was more than he'd got from the people he'd been brought up to think of as family.

He glanced at the large home on the opposite headland. At this late hour there were no lights on. The owner was probably asleep. He hadn't come to the party like everyone else within a thirty-minute radius.

But then Vassili Petrakis hadn't spoken to him since the day he'd kicked Adoni out of his house. The day he'd told him he had no right to the Petrakis name or fortune.

The name Adoni had kept, for he had no other. The lack of fortune had been a blessing in disguise, spurring him to succeed on his own. His only real regret was never seeing the boys he'd grown up thinking of as brothers. They were old enough now to decide if they wanted to see him, but Adoni wouldn't go behind the old man's back to initiate the connection.

Mouth firming, Adoni swung round, surveying his new house. It was innovative, modern, yet with a nod to local traditions.

Vassili probably hated it. Just as he hated Adoni, the living proof his first wife had played him for a fool.

Good. Adoni hoped the old man got gut-ache every time he looked across the bay.

He breathed deep, inhaling the scents of sea salt, wild herbs and something that surely was the very bones of the earth, unique to this place. Instantly he felt calmer. Though he'd lived most of his early years in the city, this stretch of coast was the home of his heart.

What did Alice think of it? She'd seemed fascinated by the scenery and openly admiring of the house.

Adoni's brow scrunched. Did it matter what she thought? She was only here while they sorted out their child's future. And till he was sure she was strong enough to look after herself.

Though now he thought about it, he didn't like the idea of her returning to that cramped bedsit and long hours at the café. Not while she carried his child.

He'd wanted to go after her this evening when she'd left the party. But his housekeeper had reported Alice had decided to turn in.

Their conversation could wait till tomorrow. But something, whether being back in Greece, in the place that felt like home, or bringing Alice into his private space, left him unsettled.

He stalked through to the master suite that had been finished in his absence. Not bothering to turn on the light, he crossed the vast space, passing the comfortable bed, the newly acquired artwork on the opposite wall and the couple of lounge chairs grouped by the window. The enormous glass door slid silently open and he stepped out onto the cantilevered deck suspended above the bluff.

Another deep breath, another draught of clear air that tasted of the earth and the sea. He didn't know why he felt so restless.

A sound made him whirl.

At the far end of the balcony was a pale glimmer. A glimmer that resolved itself into long, slender legs and some short, pale garment as Alice unfolded herself from a chair.

It seemed his housekeeper had put her in the one guest room near his own, assuming Alice was his lover.

It was an understandable assumption. Yet Adoni cursed under his breath as he took in Alice's bare arms and legs, the cloud of dark hair around her shoulders. Her nightdress, held up by narrow ribbon straps, ended high on her thighs.

As if reading his thoughts, she tugged at the hem, curving her shoulders down as if trying to find another few centimetres of cloth to cover her legs.

Her shapely, inviting legs. Silky too—he remembered the feel of them under his palm, their softness as he'd lifted her thighs around his hips as he thrust into her.

Adoni swallowed, surprised how difficult that simple act was. His throat was tight and his tongue thick. In his belly energy whooshed like a match igniting a gas oven. Sure enough, his temperature rocketed as he took in the graceful lines of her limbs and her breasts pushing against her short nightgown.

She crossed her arms as if cold and the movement hoisted the hemline even higher. Did she wear panties or was she naked beneath the flimsy fabric?

His pulse chugged hard around his body, thrumming at his temple as all the urges he'd suppressed around Alice roared back into life. The need to touch, taste, inhale the sweet fragrance of her skin. To test again the lush softness of her feminine core with the hardness rearing even now between his thighs.

Could she see his arousal? Was that why her breasts rose and fell so jerkily?

'What are you doing here?' She sounded out of breath, genuinely surprised. As if she hadn't been waiting for him.

Once again Adoni was torn between believing she was the woman she purported to be and the idea she connived at his undoing, as Dawlish warned. Just as his mother had fooled Vassili Petrakis.

Yet more and more he harboured doubts about that scenario. And there was no doubt Alice carried his child.

The idea, which should direct his mind to legalities, instead fired his rampant libido.

His gaze dropped to the fabric covering her abdomen.
There was something primal and sexy about the notion
Alice was pregnant with his baby. That her svelte body
grew ripe with his seed.

Heat flashed, searing away all thoughts except the need
he'd repressed too long. The need to touch her. To relive
the bliss he'd found in her body. Memories of that night
had haunted him ever since, and not merely because of
the pregnancy.

'It's my house, remember?' His voice was tight and low,
grinding past cramped vocal cords. 'I came to look at the
view.' And hadn't he got an eyeful? He couldn't rip his gaze
away. 'I thought you'd be in bed.'

He imagined her sprawled there, beneath him, as responsive and delectable as she'd been in London.

Adoni took a step forward, then another.

Part of his brain screamed that he'd be crazy to get involved with a woman he didn't trust. But he didn't care.

Through all the emotional tangle of discovering he was
going to be a father one thing had remained implacably certain—that Alice triggered something more intense, more
primitively needy than he'd ever felt. Right now, right here,
he gave up fighting it.

'I had trouble sleeping.'

Adoni moved, close enough to see how she swallowed,
her face lifting towards his.

'Adoni?' Her voice was sharp but he was damned if he
heard fear. It was something else. Something, if he wasn't
mistaken, remarkably close to the urgency that swept him.

Alice stepped back, straight into a chair. It scraped
across the balcony, loud in the humming silence.

Abruptly she dropped her arms to her sides, flexing
her fingers. 'What do you want, Adoni? It's too late to
discuss—'

'Who said anything about talking?'

Her breath hissed. 'I don't understand.' Her head jerked higher, the line of her jaw sharp in the moonlight. 'You brought me to Greece to discuss our baby's future. Of course we're going to talk.'

Adoni lifted his hand to stroke the soft wave of dark hair cascading over her shoulder. It felt like rippling satin. Slowly he lifted her hair to his face, bending so he could inhale the evocative scent of orange blossom.

Instantly his body was in lockdown, each muscle and tendon tense with the force required not to haul her up and plunder her mouth—and more.

'We'll talk, tomorrow.' The words grated out. 'But now it's not words I want. It's you. *Se thelo.*'

CHAPTER TEN

ALICE'S BRAIN SHORTED as thousands of volts jolted through her. Her legs trembled when Adoni buried his face in her hair, his big body so close heat radiated out, encompassing her.

She recognised desire from that night in London. It quaked through her. Just like when she'd watched Adoni dance. Others had danced too, arms extended, lunging and leaping, but she'd noticed only him.

He'd done something to her from the start. It was more than attraction, stronger than desire. She had no vocabulary for it except, perhaps, need.

Was it because he'd introduced her to sex so she was conditioned now to respond to him? Except, if it were just sex, why did she want to discover everything about Adoni? Why had she been so eager for information about him from tonight's guests?

Abruptly Adoni lifted his head, his eyes on hers, and the breath escaped her lungs in a rush.

'I want you, Alice.'

It was a statement, bold and direct. Yet surely a question too, for he didn't move a muscle. She felt tension in the air, transfixing her.

Or maybe it was her wayward body refusing to be sensible and retreat. Surely if she moved he'd release her?

Except she didn't want to retreat. She shut her eyes and felt the ripple of excitement spread to her breasts, peaked and full against her nightie, to her womb and the damp place between her legs, right down to her toes and even up to her ears. Her body was one eager erogenous zone, twanging and shivering in anticipation of his touch.

'And you want me.'

Her eyes snapped open. In this light she couldn't make out the colour of his eyes, but there was no mistaking the intensity of that glittering gaze.

Alice couldn't even think of lying. The truth had haunted her since the night they'd met.

'Yes.'

The word came on a huge sigh of relief. Pride and fear had made her try to hide it but it was undeniable.

'Well, then.' Adoni's mouth kicked up in a smile that jolted through her. 'Let's not waste any more time.'

He scooped her up, one arm at her back, the other beneath her bare legs, and strode back the way he'd come. As he stepped into a large shadowy bedroom, Alice wondered if she'd left her common sense behind on the balcony. But she didn't care. She'd never wanted anything so much.

He lowered her to the floor beside the bed. In almost the same movement his hands swept up, collecting her threadbare old nightie and briskly, ruthlessly whipping it up over her head.

Alice's breath snagged in surprise. Automatically she slid one arm across her breasts, the other hand down to the V between her legs.

Adoni's chest rose and fell abruptly, as if he couldn't get his breath. He said something she didn't catch, something in Greek that buzzed along her skin like swarming bees, soft yet dangerous.

It took everything she had to stand, facing that intense stare. But she wanted him, so badly.

'Why hide such a beautiful body?'

She opened her mouth to say she'd never bared herself to any man except him, and then he'd held her, not stood, surveying her. But she bit her tongue. He wouldn't believe that.

How could she want to give herself to a man who distrusted her?

Yet she did. Especially when he gently tugged her arms wide and sighed his pleasure, his eyes devouring her.

Adoni wasn't an ogre. Look at the way he'd cared for her, twice, when faced with her morning sickness.

Now, instead of embarrassment, Alice felt a surge of power and pride, reading his dazzled expression and the faint tremor in those hard hands. His gaze dropped to her stomach and he planted one large palm gently there, where deep inside their baby nestled.

This time the throb of sensation passing through her was pure emotion. A mix of feelings she couldn't untangle, but awe was there at the miracle they'd created, and delight as she read the same in his face.

Warmth spread, a desire to protect and nurture, not just her child but, to her amazement, the man before her. It was akin to the need she'd felt to cuddle him close when he'd spent himself inside her and, for a few precious moments, collapsed in a gasping huddle on top of her.

'You've got too many clothes on,' she murmured.

Adoni blinked, then one corner of his mouth tipped up in a half smile that almost took her out at the knees. His hold on her arms tightened, holding her steady.

'Then you'd better help me.' He drew her right hand to his belt, one wicked eyebrow lifting in challenge. His hands went to his shirt, speedily undoing buttons.

Alice should have felt conspicuous, standing naked with her hand on his belt. But she didn't. She drew the leather through the buckle with a flick, pushed the tongue of the buckle free and dragged the belt undone.

In her peripheral vision she saw the hard, shadowy planes of his chest emerge as his hands raced down the buttons, tugging his shirt free. Alice didn't let herself get distracted. Instead she grabbed his trousers, her knuckles brushing hot flesh that retracted at her touch. A shiver shook Adoni.

Delighted, she wrangled the unfamiliar fastening undone, tugging the zip low, brushing the length of his mighty erection.

Another flinch, this time a shudder, and a hiss of breath from above her.

'*Se hriazome.*'

'I don't understand Greek.' But she understood the message of his aroused body. Alice watched, her insides spiralling into ever tighter coils of want, as he shucked his shoes, thrust down his trousers and boxers, then bent to strip away his socks.

'*Se thelo*. I want you.'

The fire in her veins turned into a roaring inferno as she surveyed him, proud and utterly masculine, strong lines of bone and taut muscle.

'*Se hriazome*. I need you.' His voice burred across her skin, pulling it tight as goose bumps erupted everywhere.

Alice had seen her share of naked males, but they were all on the pages of art books or safely cast in bronze or carved from stone. She'd thought she remembered Adoni's body from that night in London but memory didn't do justice to his magnificence.

She shuffled back, overwhelmed. Surely she shouldn't feel so…overcome?

'Alice?' That deep voice held a new note. 'You're not scared?'

Scared? She was petrified!

She swallowed, her throat constricting. It didn't make sense. He wasn't going to hurt her.

Every part of her clamoured for the pleasure he promised. It wasn't as if they hadn't already done this.

Yet…

His hands curled into fists at his sides and Alice forced

her gaze up to his face, as perfect and imposing as the rest of him. 'You cried that night in London, after we had sex. Did someone hurt you?'

The only man who'd hurt her was Adoni when he'd turned on her. But surprisingly his words settled her.

Sex, that was what this was. What they'd shared in London. Only sex. Nothing to be frightened of.

For a moment there, dumbstruck by the sight of him and the strange feelings making her heart career wildly, she'd feared this might be something else. Something far more dangerous. Her heart still hammered at the idea.

'Alice?' Even in the gloom she made out the tense bulge of muscle and sinew.

'Nothing's wrong. You're just a bit daunting.' Better she share that than the fact that obliterated everything else—that she *felt* more for Adoni than she should.

Yet, instead of smiling or puffing out his chest with male pride, Adoni stood still, watching her.

'You're safe with me, Alice. I swear it.' The words, slow and deliberate, were a pledge.

She quivered and rubbed her hands up her arms, suddenly too aware that she was stark naked.

'If you want to go back to your room I promise not to follow you.'

Alice couldn't help it; her gaze dropped to the impressive rampant erection pointing directly at her belly like some heat-seeking missile locked on its target.

Adoni's rusty chuckle surprised her. 'I don't say it will be easy, but I can do it. If you want.'

The weight of his words filled the silence. She looked up, read the truth in his expression.

'I'll stay.' She had no choice. Her feet were clamped to the floor. Leaving without feeling that beautifully sculpted body against hers would be criminal.

'Good.' He reached out and snagged her hand, pressing his mouth to her palm. His tongue swiped her skin.

Immediately her nipples budded as sparks showered from her hand through her body, coalescing into a searing arc of fire that shot to the aching, empty place between her legs.

Alice shuddered and moved closer, only to halt when Adoni gripped her hips and dropped to the floor before her. Eyes huge, she watched as he bent low, his mouth skimming the skin below her navel.

His hand splayed across her belly. 'I can't describe how it makes me feel, knowing you're cradling our child.'

Another gentle kiss then another, his hands holding her close.

'Try,' she whispered. 'How does it make you feel?' Adoni hadn't spoken about anything but practicalities, about paternity and obligations. What did he *feel* about this child they'd made?

'Humble.' He planted a kiss near her hip. As well as his soft lips, she felt delicious friction where his stubble had begun to grow.

'Excited.' Another kiss, further across her belly. 'Determined.' His lips skimmed wider, trailing heat across her abdomen as if he spun a web of delicate sensation with each caress. 'Nervous.'

Alice looked down at his dark head bowed over her pale skin and her heart went into free fall. There was more honesty between them now, more true feeling than there had ever been.

She threaded her fingers through his crisp hair, intending to turn his head up so she could meet his eyes.

Instead Adoni ducked lower, sitting back on his heels, his gaze fixed on the triangle of darkness at the apex of her thighs.

Alice breathed shakily, vulnerable and needy at the

same time. Then her thoughts frayed as he lifted his hand.
His finger traced a line down through dark hair, slipping
through her folds. Sparks ignited again and she shuddered.
Internal muscles grabbed hard, more than ready for him.
Yet Adoni took his time, tracing that sensitive bud then
sliding his finger lower, deeper.

Alice gasped, her hips jerking as this time her muscles
had something to tighten on.

'Please.' Did she whisper it aloud or was the word in
her head?

Adoni didn't look up. He moved closer, grasping her
thigh and pushing it wide. Then his mouth was on her, his
tongue, and Alice was sure she'd collapse as a fierce tug
of erotic pleasure juddered through her.

Surely it was only his hands on her thighs keeping her
upright?

'Adoni? I can't...' Her voice was blurred, almost non-
existent, like the shimmer of heat over boiling water.

He pulled back and everything inside her gave a throb
of loss. Tremors ran through her and her legs shook so
hard it was a wonder her teeth didn't chatter. His eyes
met hers and something zapped between them. The air
felt different—charged, and her nostrils flared at the rich
scent she'd only smelled once before—pheromones and
sex. Arousal.

Adoni rose on his knees, hands still on her hips, and
pushed her back. Unresisting, she went, surprised to find
the mattress immediately behind her. She'd forgotten the
bed was there.

Alice opened her eyes and her arms at the same time,
ready to hold him as he sank down on her. But he held back,
kneeling on the floor between her open legs while she was
supine on the bed.

'No.' One warm hand skimmed her stomach, making
her quiver. 'This time I want to see all of you when you

come for me.' The low words in that gravel and velvet voice thrilled her.

Adoni's eyes held hers as he anchored his hands on her hips and slid her closer to the edge of the mattress. Closer to him, for in the same movement she felt him against her, then entering, then gliding hard and high within her.

Alice caught her breath, her teeth biting her bottom lip at the wonder of them together, made all the more intense by Adoni's unwavering stare.

'Does that hurt?' He was withdrawing when she leaned up, reaching for his arm.

'No, don't! It doesn't hurt. It just feels—' He moved within her again, just a smidgeon, and her eyelids fluttered.

'Good?' His mouth stretched into what might have been a smile but looked more like pain.

'Better than good.' Her hand trailed his forearm, rigid muscle and soft hair, as she flopped back on the bed.

He moved again, sure and slow, and Alice thought she'd die of pleasure. Adoni kept one hand planted possessively at her hip but he used his other hand to stroke fingers up her side to her breast, circling the nipple till she gasped and writhed, lodging him more firmly at her core. Then his caress slid low, back to her belly, circling the place where their child rested.

A force swelled within her, hard and compelling as she watched him watching her, felt the oh-so-gentle sweep of his fingertips, a counterpoint to the steady, demanding invasion of his body. Her skin tightened, there was a moment of absolute perfect stillness as his gaze devoured her. Then he muttered something guttural and urgent in Greek, his next thrust hard and true, and her body erupted in bright flames.

Alice was soaring high, jerking and arching in release, when he moved forward, propping himself over her on powerful arms.

He was still too far away. Even as she clamped around him and released with ever-diminishing strength, Alice wanted more. She wanted his chest against hers, his arms around her. His head buried at her neck or his lips on hers. She wanted to wrap her arms around him and not let go.

She wanted them to be *together*.

'Please.' She grabbed his shoulders, curling needy fingers around his smooth, rounded flesh, and tugged.

For a second more he held back, before lying like a living blanket over her—hot, silky flesh with a scattering of crisp chest hair.

Alice took her hands from his shoulders and slid her arms around his ribs, squeezing tight. Then Adoni lowered his lips to her throat, lavishing moist kisses across hypersensitised flesh so she shuddered as the dying embers of pleasure sparked anew.

He shifted between her open thighs, the angle of his penetration changing, stealing her breath all over again.

Was it crazy? This leap of the heart as they melded into one being?

Yes, it was sex, simple physical coupling. But there was more too. Something about being this near to Adoni, his heart thundering against hers, his breath sharp and humid on her skin. One strong arm tucked under her hips to angle her for his pleasure, but the other cordoned her as close as if they were one.

Adoni dipped down to kiss a trail to her breast. Then his mouth settled on her nipple, dragging it hard into his mouth as he withdrew and thrust into her. The harder he sucked, the quicker his tempo, till her blood sprinted in her arteries, her breath ragged as she strived to match his rhythm.

It wasn't enough. She lifted a leg, anchoring around his hip, and was rewarded by a growl of approval that aroused her almost as much as what he was doing to her body. Alice slid her other leg high, jostled against him as she curved her calf over him and locked her ankles.

Adoni lifted his head, his eyes dark as he powered into her, his mouth a flat line of concentration. When he loosened his grip Alice almost protested, except he slid his hand down her belly to the place where they joined and pressed hard on that sensitive nub.

One thrust, their bodies moving as one. Another. And on the third Alice's hands curled in hard, like talons against the slippery satin of his back. She arched her head back and screamed his name, feeling the writhing force swirl and rise and explode so hard she shattered. Ecstasy took her, sharpening every sense. So when he jerked, spine bowing, a stream of words tumbling from his lips as he ejaculated in throbbing waves, Alice felt everything with exquisite clarity.

They clung through the aftershocks, cradling, soothing, as if afraid to pull away.

At least that was how it felt to Alice.

Maybe it was like this every time with Adoni.

She was so wrung out, teetering even now, as if on the brink of a great height, she wondered if it was possible to pass out from pleasure.

'Are you okay?' The words feathered against her neck. She felt the shape of them more than heard them. He cleared his throat. 'Alice?'

'Yes. Fine.' Part of her, the only part with any energy left to expend, silently laughed.

If that's fine, what's good like?

'Too heavy.' His words sounded slurred as his muscles tensed, ready to move.

'No! Stay.' Alice wanted to remain like this as long as she could. She felt joined, not just physically but mentally. She and Adoni together were somehow greater than they were separately.

He gently kissed her chin, half propping himself on one elbow to take some of his weight but not moving away.

Well-being hummed through Alice. Pleasure, contentment. And when he kissed her again, lingering as if addicted to the taste of her, something far more profound consumed her.

She felt as if she belonged.

Pink and apricot streaks of sunlight brightened the dawn sky when Adoni caressed her awake. She'd stretched, slow and cautious, feeling the unfamiliar sensations in her body after last night's lovemaking. But they hadn't stopped her responding enthusiastically.

Now, after a long, satisfying and educational bout of foreplay, Alice gasped as Adoni finally filled her. She arched her back, feeling the depth of his possession in every rioting pleasure point. Hands and knees sinking a little into the mattress, she pushed back just as he moved against her from behind and drew a low groan of pleasure from him.

The sound made her heady with pleasure. *She* made him feel like that. Nor was her satisfaction just from a sense of power. She wanted him to enjoy his own release. She'd had her own climax this morning. It was his turn.

Yet as she slowly found and met his rhythm, felt the needy grasp of his hand at her hip and his other at her breast, excitement zinged through her. She'd always assumed sex in this position would be all about a guy's pleasure, not the woman's. She'd been wrong.

For when Adoni had turned her over onto her stomach and lifted her hips, driving into her with a power that rocked her on her knees, she'd waited to feel used. Instead, with his shaky hands, so at odds with the determined rhythm of his body, he worshipped and caressed. She felt his dominance but at the same time every breath, every shudder proclaimed his need for her.

Everything he did with her in bed made her feel glorious.

Adoni's breath was hot on the back of her neck as his pace picked up, his thighs jolting against her with each quick thrust. Alice lifted one hand from the bed and covered his hand, pressing it harder against her breast. Over the thud of her pulse she heard his breath hiss. That smooth rhythm fractured as he shuddered, and she bit down on a smile.

Then his hand at her hip slid down to her slick centre on his next thrust. She felt teeth graze the place where her neck met her shoulder and abruptly her self-satisfaction disintegrated. Out of nowhere, rapture took her, sucking her under just as it took Adoni. The bright morning light cracked into a thousand shards of brilliance.

Afterwards Alice lay spent. Adoni drew the sheet over her and all but vaulted out of bed. She wondered at his energy as her eyes slid shut. Was it pregnancy that made her so lethargic, or the unaccustomed sex?

She listened to the shower and wished she had the strength to get up and join Adoni. Exhausted as she was, she longed to explore his body again. Who knew what possibilities there'd be as she slicked soap over him?

Not that he'd invited her to join him but—

Why would he? You've already given him what he wants.

Did she really think anything had changed? He didn't believe she'd been a virgin. He believed she'd slept with David for money. He probably thought she'd put out because that was what women did—gave men sex to get what they wanted.

Because, tellingly, despite his sometimes protective attitude, Adoni had never retracted that allegation. It hovered between them, making her feel sullied when she thought of it.

He probably thinks last night was you softening him up for the discussion you're due to have about the baby.

Alice jack-knifed up in the bed and clamped a hand to her mouth, horror filling her. Could that be true? Her gaze fixed on the bathroom door.

After all they'd shared Adoni hadn't kissed her or touched her before getting out of bed. He hadn't uttered a word. Suddenly that seemed important.

For the first time this week nausea churned through her. But it wasn't morning sickness.

Desperately Alice replayed last night's events. Adoni had spoken of wanting her, needing her, that was all. There'd been mutual pleasure, but maybe that was about masculine pride in ensuring his partner was satisfied.

And the pang of delight and emotion that had ploughed through her when he'd spoken of their baby, kissed her belly and made love to her so wondrously?

Alice gnawed her lip.

Her emotions were unbalanced with pregnancy hormones. She'd believed Adoni had begun to feel something for her, mirroring her own growing feelings for him.

Yet there was no evidence of that. He felt strongly about the baby and he'd been kind when she was sick. But he'd brought her across a continent, far from any friends who'd help her stand up to him, when it was time to clinch a deal on their child's future. At the very first opportunity he'd seduced her, taken her into his bed as easily as if it was to be expected, not the momentous turning point it had been for her.

Alice's legs were appallingly wobbly when she planted her feet on the floor and stood.

Behind her water still gushed in the bathroom. Her revelation had taken mere minutes.

Stumbling, swerving to grab her faded old nightdress from the floor, she made her way via the terrace to her room. Now the elation had ebbed she felt stiff and achy, and more miserable than she'd been in weeks.

They'd had sex only because Adoni believed her to be available...easy.

She'd never felt so *used*. So sullied. So stupid.

Carefully she locked the doors to both the balcony and the hall, then crept into the bathroom.

She didn't want to see Adoni for a long, long time.

CHAPTER ELEVEN

ADONI ENDED HIS long-distance phone call and scowled.

Originally he'd planned to spend the morning inspecting the newly completed house instead of dealing with a work crisis.

Some things here still needed finalising. It would have been easier to bring in a top building team, especially given the architect's challenging design. Adoni's choice to use locals, specifically young workers still developing their skills, under strict supervision, had puzzled many.

But Adoni knew what it was like to be young and without resources, fighting for a toehold in a career.

Shoving his chair back from the desk, he prowled to the picture window looking over the sea.

His restlessness wasn't because he'd been side-tracked by work. It was because Alice had derailed him.

Waking beside her this morning, he'd quickly re-evaluated his plans and decided a few more hours in bed would suit him fine. Even thinking about it now tightened his jeans across his crotch. She had that effect on him.

But she'd been exhausted, reminding him of how delicate she'd looked in England, and how recently she'd been ill. He'd torn himself away, deciding a shower would give Alice time to recuperate before they took their pleasure again.

But on his return she'd disappeared. She hadn't even knocked on the door to say she was going, and when he'd gone to her room the door was locked!

Adoni rolled his head to one side, easing stiff neck muscles.

He couldn't figure her out. Alice had been willing. More

than willing. The way she'd come apart at his touch! The way she'd opened herself to him, giving him all he'd demanded and more than he'd expected…

He froze, his mind jammed by the memory of her gasping out her pleasure then wrapping herself around him, hauling him close with arms and legs locked at his hips. She'd held him so tight his control disintegrated. He'd lost track of where he ended and she began.

It had felt profound in a way sex never had.

They had felt different.

Because she was pregnant with his child?

That had to be why.

He glanced at his watch. Almost midday. He'd been caught up in work for hours. It was time he found Alice and talked about the future.

Then he could get to the bottom of why she'd run.

He found her, eventually, by the infinity pool at the end of the cantilevered deck. But she wasn't swimming or sunning herself. She was with one of the young workmen Adoni remembered from a previous site visit. They were huddled, heads together, beyond and below the stone-flagged terrace, where the land dropped away suddenly.

'What are you doing?' Adoni scowled as anger shafted through him. What was the guy doing so close to Alice?

Two heads yanked up as if pulled by strings. The youth looked nervous but Alice just tilted her head in query, eyebrows arched. She wore faded denim shorts that rode high on her slim legs as she crouched, and a sleeveless blue shirt tied at the waist. Sunlight turned her hair from dark to verging on auburn. When she moved russet highlights glinted seductively.

Something inside Adoni rolled over. She looked fresh as dew, except for a hint of tiredness around her eyes and a smudge of dirt on her chin. It was all he could do not to vault off the terrace and gather her up.

Had he ever felt this way about a woman? He tried to remember such a visceral response to Chryssa, his ex-fiancée, and failed. He'd felt desire and pride but his heart hadn't thumped out of control at the sight of her. Nor had he ever seen her dressed so simply. Chryssa had always worn expensive clothes and immaculate make-up. After they made love she'd hurry to the bathroom to primp and tidy her hair. No lying about in an abandoned tangle of bodies like Alice and he had done last night.

'Fixing the pool pump.' Her tone was cool.

'Sorry?' Adoni blinked and tried to focus. The guy with Alice got to his feet, putting a few steps between them, but she remained hunkered where she'd been. She was facing the motor and other workings for the pool, hidden beneath the edge of the flagged terrace where he stood.

'Fixing the pool pump. It wasn't installed properly but it's like the one on the estate in Devon.'

Adoni stared. He'd never pictured Alice doing pool maintenance. Had running the estate in Devon been that hands-on? He knew so little about her.

Alice turned to the youth. 'Here, Costa. Like this.' She beckoned him closer and with one darting look at Adoni the kid approached. She fiddled with something then sat back. 'Try it now.' The boy leaned forward, made an adjustment and the motor hummed into life. The kid beamed at Alice, then seeing Adoni's expression, wiped the smile off his face and quickly moved away.

'Thank you, miss.'

'No problem. I'm glad to help.' She rose and dusted off her hands and knees, watching the youth move away, presumably to report to his supervisor who was overseeing the final jobs on site.

Alice watched him go then turned to Adoni, her expression shuttered. 'What's wrong? You look angry.'

Adoni leaned over and offered his hand. He *was* angry, and it unsettled him.

The hot rush of blood to the head when he'd seen Alice with another man had taken him by surprise. They might not be committed to each other, but she'd been in his bed mere hours ago. That had to explain the raw possessiveness priming his body to high alert. Adrenaline buzzed in his blood as if in preparation to fight a rival.

Finally her smaller hand touched his and he firmed his fingers around it, hauling her up till they stood toe to toe.

'Adoni?' She tilted her head to one side, reading his face, then abruptly she stepped away, ripping her hand free. Her nostrils flared in anger even as something that looked like hurt tightened her face. 'You thought I was coming on to him, didn't you?' Her eyes grew huge in her pale face. 'That's the sort of woman you think I am.'

'No, it wasn't like that.' He hadn't thought she'd instigated anything. He'd wanted to *protect* her. Did she have any idea how alluring she looked with her bare limbs and sweet curves?

'Yeah, right.' She marched over to pick up a book he hadn't noticed beside one of the sun loungers.

Adoni followed, determined to convince her, when a picture on an open page caught his eye. It was a sketchbook and even from a couple of metres the delicate work in it looked exquisite.

'What's that?'

Alice looked down. 'A drawing.'

'*You* did that?' He thought back to her threadbare bedsit with those wonderful botanical studies, so perfect and so out of place in such drab surroundings. Were they Alice's? He'd thought them done by a professional.

'Yes, I did.' She dropped the book onto the lounger and turned, hands on hips. Her breasts rose as she sucked in a deep breath. 'What's wrong? You think *gold-diggers* can't draw?' Fire flashed in her eyes, lightening them from dark slate to something more vibrant. 'You think we're so busy seducing every man we meet we don't have time for—'

'Stop it!' He closed his hands around her upper arms, yanking her against him. How had they got to this when hours ago they'd been locked together in bliss? His gut twisted at her jarring words and the whisper of guilt they evoked. For he had accused her, hadn't he? He couldn't remember if he'd called her a gold-digger but he'd said something similar.

'I won't stop it.' Her chin angled defiantly. 'It's what you're thinking, isn't it?'

'No, it's not.'

He felt a mighty shudder run through her, saw her teeth sink into her bottom lip as if to stop it trembling and watched pain shadow those accusing eyes.

Adoni wanted to slam his mouth down on hers. He wanted to expunge the hurt he saw in her face and rewind the clock to this morning, when they'd been in bed. The day had gone downhill since he'd left her there. He should have stayed. Of course if he had they'd probably still be having sex. They might have stayed there all day. Yet now Alice hissed at him like a wounded animal, her eyes huge and accusing.

He could kiss her into silence, maybe even into his bed. But that would solve nothing.

Except to relieve that burn in his groin.

You want her again, don't you? Even when she's fighting and spitting at you.

'I said, let me go.' She pulled, trying to free her arms. Adoni had to force himself not to tighten his hold. Brute strength wasn't the way.

He let her go, holding his hands up in a placating gesture. 'It's not what you think, Alice.'

'Sure.' He hated the cynicism in her tone almost as much as the pain in her eyes and crumpled mouth.

'We need to talk.'

'About the baby, I know.' She gathered the sketchbook and a leather pouch he assumed held pencils and clutched them to her chest as if for protection.

Guilt was a corkscrew drilling through him. It was true that in the beginning he'd thought the worst, primed by Dawlish's information. But it was a long time since he'd felt that way. He knew Alice better now. She wasn't a cardboard cut-out villainess. He wouldn't have taken her into his bed last night if she were.

But he'd never told her that, had he?

'Not the baby. That can wait.' Her stunned gaze locked on his. He surprised himself too, for he needed to secure his child's future. But this was overdue. 'We need to clear the air first.'

Which was how Alice found herself beside Adoni in the vast lounge room that hung out over the sea. Their chairs, so comfortable it was like being cradled, were drawn up together as if they were friends enjoying the spectacular view together.

But Alice couldn't relax, nor let herself be lulled by the scenery or the quiet luxury. She watched Adoni take a sip of coffee from a tiny cup then place it on a side table. It struck her that he didn't look as sure of himself as usual.

Alice ignored the porcelain teapot beside her and the tantalising aroma of the brew within it. Instead she watched Adoni. The thick glass windows protected from the midday heat but didn't dim the sunlight. Her heart sank as her gaze traced his profile. He was impossibly, arrogantly gorgeous, enough to make her heart trip.

'You're wrong, Alice. I don't think you're a gold-digger.'

'You implied it.' She sat straighter. 'No, you *said* it, even if not in those words.'

'I'd never intentionally take such a woman into my bed. So how do you explain last night?'

His gaze bored into hers and she shrugged, the movement jerky. 'Maybe you weren't thinking with your head.'

That surprised a laugh out of him and, to her horror, the warmth of it coursed through her like hot syrup, making her shift in her seat.

'You could be right.' Suddenly his expression sobered. 'But, for the record, I'd never have slept with you if I thought that. Or brought you into my home.'

Alice stared into those beautiful eyes and wished she could tell if it were true. 'Then why accuse me in the first place? I know you were shocked about the pregnancy, but I was too. That was no excuse. You were so ready to believe the worst gossip about me and David.'

Adoni sat forward. 'You have to expect some response when a guy finds you rifling his wallet.'

Instantly her face flamed. She'd forgotten that. 'How did you know?' She'd left the room before he'd returned from the bathroom.

One black brow rose in a slashing line. 'You didn't put the cards back properly.'

Alice nodded. She'd been in a hurry and when she'd heard him coming she'd dropped the wallet and run for the door.

'If you'd needed money for a taxi—'

'It wasn't that. I just…' She turned and stared at the sea, noticing how the clear shallows gave way to aquamarine then the distinctive green-blue of Adoni's eyes, before deepening to a rich navy.

She turned back, thrusting aside embarrassment. 'I couldn't remember your last name.' The words tumbled out. 'You told me but all I could remember was Adoni. It seemed important that I knew your name because…' She clamped her lips shut rather than say that he'd been her first lover. She'd told him that and he hadn't believed her. 'I didn't like the idea of having sex with someone and not knowing their name.' She stared at him, defying him to laugh.

Adoni's expression was arrested. 'But why leave? Why run?'

Because she'd looked around the stunning, incredibly expensive suite and realised she didn't belong. It was only Adoni's warmth and charm, and the invitation in his eyes, that had made her forget that.

She settled for sharing part of the truth. 'I'd never had a one-night stand and I was out of my depth. I didn't know if I was expected to leave while you were in the bathroom. I didn't know the protocol.' She'd had a horror of outstaying her welcome. She'd already behaved foolishly, even if the sex had been the most wonderful thing she'd ever experienced.

Adoni shook his head. 'I was looking forward to spending the rest of the night with you.'

'Really?' Alice bit her cheek as she heard what sounded like delight in her voice. Was she so easily pleased?

But Adoni didn't seem to notice. He leaned forward, forearms braced on his thighs, hands clasped. 'I must apologise. The day you made the appointment to see me, my temporary PA mentioned you in front of Miles Dawlish.'

Alice's nape prickled. 'Let me guess. He told you about me?'

Slowly Adoni nodded. 'I realise now he had an axe to grind.'

'You can say that again.' Alice hunched her shoulders and rubbed her hands along her arms, remembering years of verbal abuse from the man, every time he'd wanted a loan from David's estate and been turned down.

'Why don't you tell me about it? About *you*. There's nothing to be gained by keeping it to yourself, is there?'

Adoni was right. By letting him believe the worst she'd only made things more difficult. Though had she *let* him? When she'd tried to explain he'd brushed her words aside. Yet once he'd made his opinion clear, her pride had dug in and she'd refused to make the effort.

This man was her baby's father. He'd be in her life from now on. Her belly clenched at the realisation.

'After all, you know about my past. There are only two other people who know the truth about my parents.'

Alice's eyes met his and she felt again that whump of sensation, a deep throb at her core. At the time she'd been moved by his revelation, but too caught up in her own concerns to really consider what it had meant for him to share that secret. It made her past problems fade. At least she'd had people who genuinely loved her.

'Okay.' He was right—it would help if he knew it all. Yet, though her life was an open book, she was reluctant. She tried to live in the present, not dwell on the past.

As she hesitated Adoni leaned forward and poured tea into the delicate porcelain cup on the table beside her, adding milk. At her raised eyebrows he murmured, 'I know how you like it.'

The words took her back to her shabby room in Devon. To Adoni prowling the tiny space like a Greek god come down from Olympus to find himself in a cramped bedsit. He'd been annoying and bossy but…kind.

'Thank you.' She lifted the cup to her lips, inhaled the fragrant steam then sipped. Instantly she felt better. She shuffled back in the chair, letting it embrace her, and turned her head to find Adoni watching her, his lips twitching. 'What?'

'You English are addicted to your tea, aren't you?'

She shrugged, glancing at the tiny cup of intensely dark coffee beside him. 'Like you Greeks and your coffee.'

He lifted his shoulders in a casual shrug that tugged at her feminine centre. It made Alice remember the power in his tall frame, and the way he'd carefully leashed it to ensure her pleasure before his own. Her gaze dipped to her tea as she fought a quiver of excitement.

'I don't have any big secrets and you know most of it.' She paused, annoyance flickering because he'd investigated her. But the investigator obviously didn't know everything. She lifted her eyes to the soothing view of sea and sky that reminded her of her happy childhood.

'I'm an only child and grew up in Cornwall. We were a close family. My mother was a talented portrait artist.'

'That's where you get your artistic talent.'

Alice felt the words sink in. It had been too long since she'd thought of herself as having real talent. She'd longed to attend art school but life and a lack of funds had got in the way. This morning was the first time in ages that she'd picked up a sketchbook.

'From my father too. He was a commercial cartoonist.' Even in his wheelchair, as his body slowly failed him, he'd worked desperately hard, trying to support them. 'His cartoons were so insightful, yet they made you laugh.'

'You're proud of him.'

'Of course.' She met Adoni's probing gaze. 'I'm proud of both of them. Not just because of their talent. They were lovely people.' She still missed them.

Alice took a fortifying sip of tea.

'We were caught in a motorway accident when I was twelve. A lorry skidded on ice and crossed several lanes to slam into us. My mother died instantly but it took ages for them to cut my father out.' Her throat closed and she pretended to take another sip.

'I'm sorry. That must have been...' He paused. 'I can't begin to imagine how hard it was.'

Alice nodded. 'Somehow it seemed worse that I came out of it with only bruising and a cracked wrist. It took a long time before I stopped feeling guilty.' It had almost felt as if it was her fault her mother had died.

She saw Adoni's hand move as if to touch her, then he pulled back. Alice was grateful. Talking about this still choked her up.

'After that we had to give up the house in Cornwall because Dad was in a wheelchair and couldn't cope with the stairs.' And because money had been so tight they couldn't afford the mortgage. 'An old friend of my parents offered us a place in Devon. It was ideal, on one floor and with doorways wide enough for Dad's chair.'

Alice turned to Adoni. 'David Bannister was my godfather. He and his wife saw my mother's work when she was a student and encouraged her. She sold her first painting to them.' She paused, waiting, but Adoni's expression was unreadable.

'David was very good to us. More than a landlord, he was a friend, and we needed all we could get.' Her mother's death had strained relations with their only relatives. Her mother's sister had blamed Alice's father for the accident, despite the evidence. There'd been a rift between the families ever since, till Alice's cousin Emily had invited her to attend the wedding.

'Dad's injuries were complicated. His condition worsened till eventually he couldn't work. Then David waived our rent and there was always a basket of fresh produce from the estate or our neighbours. We lived in the artists' colony you saw.'

'No wonder Jasper is so protective.'

She shrugged. 'Everyone pitched in together.' Alice drew a deep breath. 'Dad fought his health problems but he died when I was seventeen. Soon after, David asked me to come and live at the big house.'

Alice turned narrowed eyes on Adoni, waiting for a re-action, but he merely nodded.

'He was a widower and missed his wife dreadfully. He said he was lonely rattling around by himself. But he did it for me. So *I* wouldn't be alone.' Her lips tightened as she remembered the lies Adoni had believed. Her stomach churned in indignation. 'For the record we were never lovers. He didn't seduce me. He was like a grandfather or an uncle.'

'It was good you had someone to care for you when your father died.' There was no doubt in Adoni's deep voice, just statement of fact.

Alice dipped her head in agreement. 'It wasn't supposed to be long-term. I was researching art schools. I wanted to go as soon as I could, after I'd worked to save enough money. David was talking of giving me an interest-free loan. But then he was diagnosed with a degenerative illness.'

She reached for her tea, taking a long drink as she remembered her devastation. 'He was upbeat, said the treatment would help. But it didn't work as well as hoped and he needed assistance sooner than expected.

'In the beginning he urged me to leave, but I refused. I wanted to be there for him, as he'd been for us.' Sometimes she wondered if she'd clung to him so desperately because he was the one person who'd always been there.

'As he grew worse, he relied on me more and more. He didn't advertise his illness, didn't want people feeling sorry for him, so Miles Dawlish never knew till late. Dawlish is David's wife's nephew and, as the estate came from her family and she never had any children, he was the heir. And a bumptious little man too.'

'He is. Thoroughly unlikable.'

Alice swung round to stare. 'But you believed what he said about me.'

Adoni stared straight back. 'I didn't know he was biased. But yes, it wasn't one of my finer moments.' A flicker of a smile appeared at the corners of those mesmerising eyes, arresting Alice. 'I was out of sorts because the fascinating woman I wanted to spend the night making love to had disappeared, presumably to siphon off my credit cards.' He spread his hands. 'I'm sorry.'

She shook her head, her pulse thrumming at the admission he'd wanted to make love to her all night. As if he couldn't get enough of the passion they shared either. 'I suppose it was understandable in the circumstances.'

She took a deep breath and hurried on, eager to get this over. 'The sicker David became the more I helped. At first it was just correspondence and keeping him company but then it was running the estate.'

'Like fixing the pool?' Adoni's half smile did strange things to her insides.

'And more. Organising improvements. Checking on tenants, doing the books. That's where Dawlish and I came into conflict. David couldn't bear the guy and he kept trying to borrow money. After the first few times David refused to see him and I was the messenger.' Alice lifted one shoulder. 'That's when he turned ugly. Accused me of sleeping with David to get money.' She laughed, the sound bitter. 'Actually, most of the money was tied up in the estate, then there were charity commitments like the artists' colony. What was left over went on David's care.'

Poor David—he'd been so determined to keep some of his personal funds aside so Alice could study art. In the end she'd had to lie and pretend it hadn't been spent on palliative care, so as not to distress him.

Silence descended. Not a combative one, but a reflective one. Alice curled back in her chair and finished her tea, feeling strangely lighter.

'Thank you,' Adoni said eventually. 'I appreciate you telling me.'

She turned to find his eyes on her. She couldn't decipher his expression. 'Where does that leave us?'

'Ready to move forward.' It was a statement but she read the question in his eyes, as if he sought her agreement. Slowly she nodded.

'So now you want to talk about the baby.' She straightened her shoulders, trying to dredge up energy though she wilted after the emotions of the last half hour.

'That can wait.'

'Really?' Surely the baby's future was uppermost in his mind? It was the sole reason she was here.

'Really.' His mouth tipped up at one side in a slow smile and reaction jangled through her. He wasn't even touching her and she wanted— 'I find I have to go to Athens for business. I'll be away overnight.'

Alice fought not to show a reaction though her stomach dipped at the news. As if she didn't want him to go.

'Would you like to come? You didn't see anything of the city except the airport.' He paused. 'There's an art exhibition you might be interested in too.'

Instantly Alice nodded, delight filling her. But was it delight at the idea of seeing some of Greece's artistic wonders?

Or relief at delaying their negotiations about the future?

Perhaps it was simply because they'd cleared up the doubts and distrust between them.

Alice had a terrible suspicion her delight was because she'd be with Adoni.

CHAPTER TWELVE

ALICE BRUSHED HER hands down the delicate folds of her dress. The material was finer than anything she'd ever worn, soft as gossamer.

Initially she'd refused Adoni's charity—the gift of a dress and shoes to wear tonight. She hated being beholden. The fact he'd already paid her next month's rent was still a bone of contention. It was fine for him to contribute to their child's upbringing but *she* wasn't after his money.

It was only the realisation her holiday wardrobe contained just shorts, jeans and two well-worn summer dresses that changed her mind. Plus meeting Adoni's chic, exquisitely dressed assistant in Athens. Effie had assured her Adoni was right, that the guests at the exhibition opening tonight would be dressed to the nines.

Reluctantly Alice had been persuaded, accepting Effie's help to negotiate what she suspected were Athens' top boutiques. There were no prices on display and Alice shuddered to think how much her outfit cost. But she *had* enjoyed herself. Despite her glamorous air, Effie was fun, down-to-earth and had an eye for fashion.

Alice had never looked so good.

She twirled before the mirror, the narrow sapphire pleats of the short skirt flaring around her. The glittering fitted bodice and thin shoulder straps sparkled as if crusted with gems rather than sequins and beads. Even her shoes of sapphire silk had tiny beads on the spindly heels that winked and flashed when she moved.

Adoni couldn't ignore her dressed like *this*.

The thought speared through her before she could stop it. Not that he'd ignored her after yesterday's discussion.

He'd been…considerate. So considerate he'd left her straight after dinner, telling her he understood she must be tired, and headed to his office to work.

Alice had lain awake for hours, waiting for him to join her in her vast bed, waiting for him to make love with her again, but he hadn't. She'd woken this morning, late, and just in time for their trip to Athens, feeling out of sorts and needy.

She didn't know what worried her most, her neediness or the possibility he'd decided sex with her wasn't as satisfying as he'd expected. Had he grown tired of her?

Or was it the retelling of her past that made him pull back?

But Alice refused to feel like a victim. She fitted her one piece of good jewellery around her throat and told herself she didn't care about his withdrawal. Much.

Her hand swiped her flat abdomen. She was here to plan her child's future. And to see a little of Greece. Not to pine after Adoni.

This afternoon she'd visited the Parthenon and the Acropolis Museum, marvelling over sculptures she'd seen in books but only dreamed of viewing in person. She'd marvelled at the workmanship, the beautiful images. Yet all the time she'd been thinking of another sculpture, this one warm and supple. A living man whose honed muscles and lean strength made her pulse quicken and her insides melt.

Alice now understood the ancient Greeks' fascination with the nude male form. When that form was like Adoni's—

'Alice?' A knock sounded at her door. 'Are you ready?'

Her eyes widened in the mirror as excitement throbbed through her. Excitement and anticipation.

She'd never been to an exhibition opening. Never been out on the town, unless you counted a meal at the local pub with workmates. But the real reason for her excitement was altogether different.

She wanted Adoni.

It was foolish. They came from different worlds and would separate after they'd agreed on a plan for their baby's future. But meanwhile Alice was determined to grasp what she wanted. She had too much experience of life passing her by.

'Coming!' She spun towards the door. Her skirt flared, caressing her thighs and making her smile.

Oh, yes, she knew what she wanted.

'You look fantastic.'

Original, Petrakis. Can't you do better?

But it was true. Alice looked good enough to eat. His mouth watered at the thought of kissing his way up those bare legs and—

'So do you.' Alice's smile was wide, her eyes sparkling. Adoni hadn't seen her smile like that since the first night in London. It did crazy things to his self-control. A control undermined by the fact she didn't *look* pregnant, or like a woman who needed careful handling.

Last night, with her revelations fresh in his mind and those smudges beneath her eyes, partly because he'd kept her from sleep the night before, Adoni had avoided her bed. Just. It had been touch and go. In the end he'd spent hours testing his new gym, then doing laps in the pool, trying to burn off his hunger for her.

It had hit him anew how wrong he'd been about her. How she'd actually been a virgin when they'd met in London. Adoni remembered that night, the moment of tense stillness and shocking doubt, which he'd dismissed as an impossibility. Now, remembering it, he felt obliged to exert restraint. Alice was pregnant, inexperienced and needed rest.

How was he to keep his hands off her when she looked like this?

'Effie has great taste in clothes.'

Adoni flattened his lips rather than blurt out that it was the woman, not the clothes that dazzled.

Her hand went to her throat in a nervous gesture that belied her confident smile.

'That's a beautiful piece.' He leaned in, pretending to examine the black choker with its fiery opal centre stone. 'Expensive too.' He was speaking at random, hiding the swift inhale that dragged the scent of warm feminine skin and orange blossom deep into his lungs.

'It was an eighteenth birthday gift from Jasper, our old neighbour in Devon.' Her chin notched up in challenge. 'He's a jewellery designer.'

No mistaking her crisp tone. It confused Adoni till he remembered his earlier accusation that she lived off older men. Heat scored his cheeks, guilt biting. He was a proud man, not used to feeling in the wrong.

'He's very talented. The dark blue matches your eyes but the flashes of red and green bring it to life. It suits you— vibrant and with hidden depths.'

'Adoni?' Her head tilted to one side in that endearing way. 'I *think* that's the nicest thing you've ever said to me.'

He took her hand and kissed it, pleased at her shiver and the sudden widening of her eyes. 'The night's still young.'

'This one's intriguing. I love the unusual perspective.' Alice sounded thoughtful but with that hint of excitement he'd sensed all night. Standing beside him, her attention was on a larger-than-life portrait.

The chatter and noise of the exhibition's opening night continued, but in this corner it was muted. Perhaps it seemed so because Adoni's attention was fixed on her.

The artist, who'd followed Alice, spoke enthusiastically

about using light and perspective to reveal character. Instead of listening, Adoni watched Alice.

As if sensing his regard she flashed him a smile, then she took a half-step back, inviting him to join the discussion.

She'd been doing that all evening, favouring him with that wide smile. It dazzled more surely than the exquisite opal at her throat that flashed fire every time she moved.

Did she know how that invitation affected him? That it made him want to plough her back against one of the stark white walls and reacquaint himself with every centimetre of her svelte body?

The dancing light in her eyes suggested she did.

He'd have dragged them out of here and found relief for the hunger riding him hard, but for something else. Alice was having the time of her life.

She was in her element. It shouldn't surprise him, given her family history and her own talent. Yet Adoni was transfixed by the sheer joy she radiated, being here.

She loved the party, mingling with people, striking up conversations. Laughing over the occasional language difficulties and gamely trying out the few Greek words she'd got from who knew where.

It was like discovering a completely different woman.

No. Not that. This was the same woman whose humour and forthright attitude, and sexy body, had seduced him that first night. Who'd intrigued even when he'd railed that fate had tied him to what he'd thought was a conniving gold-digger.

He'd got in the habit of thinking of Alice in simplistic terms. First as a *femme fatale*. Then as someone needing protection. Morning sickness had made her fragile and her living conditions had appalled, making him want to take care of her.

Now he saw depths he hadn't fully appreciated.

'Adoni admired the portrait in the first room,' she told

the artist. Lightly she touched Adoni's hand and lightning shot through him, making his blood fire and his heart drum. 'The one of the old lady.' She turned to him. 'It reminded you of someone, didn't it?'

How had she known? He hadn't said anything. Add perceptive to her list of qualities.

He nodded. 'Our housekeeper when I was a boy. She looked old but when you met her eyes you realised she was young at heart.'

Memory blanketed him. Suddenly he was a scrawny kid again, always in the kitchen because meal times couldn't keep up with his growth spurts. Maria had teased him but she'd shown more warmth and understanding than he'd ever got from his mother.

Alice threaded her fingers through his and squeezed. Her dark gaze was soft with understanding.

How did she *do* that?

He didn't need understanding. His life was exactly as he wanted it.

'I think—' Alice turned to the artist '—you'd better mingle with your guests. We don't want to monopolise you.'

The guy shrugged, obviously happy basking in Alice's enthusiasm. And enjoying the delectable picture she made in that short dress.

Adoni leaned closer. 'Yes, it's important you circulate. It will help sales.'

The guy took one look at Adoni's face and agreed.

'You've got an admirer. He looked smitten.' Adoni smiled when Alice's gaze instantly left the artist and turned to *him*. Their eyes met and he felt that familiar buzz. Anticipation. Possessiveness.

It should bother him. It had been years since he'd felt proprietorial about a woman. Yet somehow—

'He was hoping for a sale, that's all.' She gave a self-deprecating smile. 'He probably thought I had the money to buy one of his works.'

Did she really not understand how attractive she was, with her elegance and vivacity?

All night she'd been a flame drawing moths as other guests responded to her. She was bright, fun and truly interested in them.

'Adoni!' A blonde socialite air-kissed him with enthusiasm then turned to Alice. 'Here he is, Alice.' She introduced a young man as an aspiring jewellery maker. 'He's interested in the artists' colony you mentioned, *and* seeing that stunning choker up close.'

Adoni watched, annoyed, as the guy moved in for a close-up view that included the top of Alice's breasts above her low-cut gown. Had her breasts always been that full or had they changed with pregnancy? Two nights ago they'd filled Adoni's hands to perfection.

He reached out to yank the guy back by the scruff of his neck when Alice's fingers caught his. Her intimate smile momentarily derailed his thoughts.

Then she freed her hand and unclipped the necklace. Handing it to the jeweller, she leaned into Adoni. 'It's the necklace he's interested in.'

Adoni merely raised one eyebrow and hauled her hard against his side, staking his claim.

For a second Alice looked surprised, then she smiled a cat-that-got-the-cream smile that made Adoni's temperature spike. If she kept looking at him like that...

Yet Adoni forced himself to be patient, not cut her evening short. There was a different sort of pleasure in being with her here.

When he'd taken Chryssa out, she hadn't engaged with others so much as thrived on their adulation as she paraded her latest expensive outfit. He'd realised too late he was a trophy to show off, a means to climb the social ladder and fund her lifestyle.

Alice, by contrast, was interested in people, vibrant and amusing as she chatted, not about herself but about them and art and a hundred other things.

Plus she responded to him as a man, a companion, not a shortcut to the good life, turning to him again and again, drawing him into the conversation.

She was as genuine as he'd first thought her. After a lifetime dealing with people whose professed love masked pride and selfishness, he appreciated how special that was.

But below that, humming through each pulse of his blood, was a demand he could no longer ignore.

Finally, after another half-hour, Adoni murmured in her ear, 'We need to leave.'

Questioning eyes met his. What she read in his face he didn't know but she blushed and her pupils dilated. He felt her shudder and her back arched to his touch as if inviting a caress.

'Now!' His voice cracked on the word. He'd stayed for her sake but if he didn't have her soon he'd combust.

'Yes.' Her whisper feathered his chin, evoking a surge of pure triumph.

Their goodbyes were rushed. No doubt everyone guessed the reason for their sudden urgency but Adoni didn't give a damn. All he cared about was Alice, wrapping his arms around her, sinking into her slick, tight body and losing his mind.

'Adoni!' Her breathy voice almost undid him as he strode out onto the pavement. 'Wait. I can't go this fast in heels.'

For answer he simply swept her up into his arms, carrying her to his sports car, just down the street. He couldn't wait for the valet to drive it up.

Her gurgling laugh caressed like warm satin, drawing nerves to the verge of breaking point. Adoni ignored the sea of faces turned towards them and within seconds they were in the car, peeling away into the traffic.

Neither said a word as he drove. Adoni was hyper-aware of Alice's every movement. Of her quickened breathing and the slide of her dress as she crossed her legs, then uncrossed them. Either she was as turned-on as he was or she was intent on driving him crazy. With every restless movement he imagined her bare leg sliding against him, up over his hip and—

'We're here.' He swung through the electric gates and up, past cypresses and colourful oleanders lining the driveway, into the garage beneath his high-set home.

Adoni switched the engine off, the only sound the tick-tick of the motor and the thud of his pulse. He drew a deep breath, willing his body to relax, but it was impossible. He was too wound-up. Clicking the remote control to shut the garage door behind them, he got out and went round to the passenger side, helping her out.

'Thank you, Adoni. I had a lovely evening.'

Her hand was small in his, her eyes bright with sapphire depths. She stood so close her breasts teased his torso. The light imprint of her body fuelled the fire burning within.

'It's not over yet.' He pulled her wrists up and over his shoulders, gripping her waist, marvelling at how perfectly its seductive curve fitted his palms. Adoni tugged and she came willingly, leaning up on her toes and planting those lush lips against his mouth.

Adoni groaned and lashed his arms round her, accepting her invitation and driving down with his tongue, plundering the velvety heat of her mouth. She tasted so impossibly good. Alice arched, supple yet taut, and a rolling wave of lust engulfed him. At this rate it would be a miracle if they made it upstairs to a bedroom.

Her fingers channelled through the hair at the back of

his scalp, sending trails of flame racing down his spine then circling round to his groin.

'Alice.' He groaned it against her mouth, desperation rising. He closed his eyes, inhaling orange blossom, motor oil and musky pheromones.

He shuddered and dragged his mouth from hers. 'We need a bed.'

Air filled his starved lungs as he snapped his eyes open and made himself step back. But he kept her prisoner with his hands. It would take a moment before he found the strength to let her go.

Heavy-lidded eyes met his. Her mouth, always out-rageously seductive, was a reddened pout, ripe from his kisses. His fingers tightened.

'I can't wait that long.'

Adoni's clothes felt far too tight, restricting. It took everything he had not to move. He shook his head, the movement straining already taut muscles. 'Don't say that or I'll forget about behaving like a civilised man and take you here, in the garage.'

She blinked, her pupils dilating, drawing his fascinated gaze. 'I don't feel very civilised, Adoni.' Her voice grew husky on his name, turning it into a caress. 'I've wanted you all night and...'

He lifted her off the floor and up against his hardness, his gaze sweeping the long garage. *There*. Just metres away—a work bench against the wall.

Adoni had just enough control to check the surface—like everything else in the property it was pristine—before he lowered her onto it. Instantly, gratifyingly, she opened her knees and he stepped in, tucked hard between her splayed thighs.

'Yes!' Her head fell back against the wall as he ground himself against her.

Adoni lifted his hand to stroke the perfect pale arch of

her throat, stunned at how erotic it was and how his hand shook. What was it about Alice that turned him on so hard and fast? The fact he'd planted his baby inside her? Yes. No. It was more than that.

There was no time to solve that riddle now. Her hands were on his belt as he shoved her floaty skirt up her bare legs. He tugged her hard against him.

She moaned and he bent, nipping at that sensitive spot where her neck curved down to her shoulder. She moaned again, ripping his trousers undone while he slipped his hand between her legs. She shuddered as he tore her panties aside and stroked her.

'No!' Her hand clamped his wrist. 'I want *you*,' she said. 'Just you.'

Adoni worked on autopilot. He wasn't conscious of anything but the expression on her face and his desperation to give her—give them both—what they needed.

He'd never been so aroused. So when he thrust, slow and sure, right to the core of her, it was no surprise when that glorious slide ended in ripples of pleasure. They grew into shudders of ecstasy, engulfing them and sending them spinning towards the stars.

Later–much later—they made it to his bedroom. Again they came together in a glorious conflagration that wrung them out and made a mockery of Adoni's belief that he knew the full measure of physical ecstasy.

Now he lay in bed with Alice curled up against him, her leg across his hips, her soft little belly, where their baby rested, pressed into his side.

Adoni just had the strength to stroke the dark tresses spilling over her shoulders.

In the distance Athens hummed, the cityscape visible through the wide windows. But his mind wasn't on the floodlit Acropolis or the network of streets. It was on the woman in his arms. And the future.

In the beginning he'd wanted only his child. To love it and give it the life it deserved.

Now Adoni wanted more.

He wanted Alice.

He breathed slowly, testing the idea.

It was crazy to want any woman long-term, given his history. Crazy after knowing her such a brief time. Yet he did, and Adoni trusted his instinct. Instinct had got him the most important breaks in his career. Instinct came through when carefully laid plans failed.

Instinct told him he wanted Alice. That he'd *keep* wanting her. This wasn't a passing attraction.

She'd make a good mother, unselfish and caring. She'd do her best for their son. For some reason Adoni was convinced it was a boy.

The more Adoni knew about Alice's story, the more he realised she took family, caring and duty seriously. She had her dream of art school but had deferred it to look after the man who'd supported her family. She paid her debts. She was honourable.

Honourable. Caring. Sexy. Even her obstinacy, her feistiness were assets, or would be when directed towards nurturing their son. And weren't two loving parents better for a child than two parents living apart, turning their child's life into a schedule of travel and disrupted routines?

More than that, there was something vital, adorable, unfettered about Alice. She was a breath of fresh air—so different from him and yet, he was discovering, so similar in the ways that mattered.

She shifted, her breath stroking his skin. His nipple tightened at that phantom caress and his loins stirred.

It was tempting to wake her again. He was insatiable. He'd told himself it was due to the child she carried. Or because she really had been a virgin when she came to him. However politically incorrect, there was something viscerally exciting about knowing he was her first lover. He could, if he wanted, be the only lover she ever had.

The idea solidified his determination. He just had to figure out how to get everything he wanted.

CHAPTER THIRTEEN

THEIR OVERNIGHT STAY in Athens became a week as Adoni worked and Alice explored, discovering and delighting in what the city had to offer. Evenings were spent dining out, enjoying the nightlife, then hurrying back to his sleek white mansion and making love into the wee hours.

Neither mentioned the future, or her leaving. It was as if they both realised this bubble of mutual delight was fragile. They didn't want to spoil it with the nitty-gritty negotiations that must eventually come.

Alice knew she should think of leaving but couldn't summon the energy. England with its dismal spring weather and her tiny, cold room seemed a million miles away.

Was it so wrong to accept Adoni's hospitality and not worry about her rent for just a little longer? As he'd said, she really was feeling better for the rest and surely a healthy mother was better for the baby?

Or maybe you're looking for excuses to stay because you can't imagine leaving him.

It was true. She didn't *want* to go.

So when Adoni presented his plan a few days after they returned to his villa in the Mani, Alice stifled her amazement and actually considered his proposition.

'We both want what's best for our baby.'

Alice nodded. 'Of course.'

Adoni smiled, distracting her as he stroked a finger down her bare arm.

They sat on the balcony outside the master bedroom, enjoying the early evening air, scented by the wildflowers that bloomed so prolifically around the house. The rhythm of waves soothed when her pulse beat hard at Adoni's touch.

One touch was all it ever took, sometimes just a look, for her to melt. Alice shivered and tried to concentrate.

'We both need to build a relationship with him.'

'Him?' Alice raised her brows but Adoni merely smiled. That wry tilt of his lips was so ridiculously attractive it stole her breath.

'What can I say? I believe our child is a boy.'

Alice said nothing. Not because of Adoni's bizarre claim, but because when he said *our child* it did strange things to her insides. As if they were a couple, a family.

The notion, like an elusive wisp of aromatic smoke, tantalised before fading into nothing. They weren't a couple; they were sharing pleasure for a short time, no strings attached.

Alice shifted in her chair, refusing to acknowledge the swift plunge of her belly that felt like disappointment.

'It will be better if he has both of us in his life, *ne*?'

'Yes.' Alice tilted her head, searching Adoni's face. His use of the Greek word *ne* for yes caught her attention. He rarely used Greek with her, except when they were naked. He reverted to his native language in the throes of passion and Alice adored it—he sounded so desperate, so out of control then. Was Adoni *nervous*?

'And we agree security is vital to a child.'

Again Alice nodded. 'Where are you going with this, Adoni?' While they hadn't formally discussed future arrangements, occasionally one or the other would remark on some aspect they believed important. It had been a relief to discover their views coincided—a good relationship with both parents. Time in both Greece and England, and raising their child as bilingual, enriched by the cultures of both parents. 'You're going over what we've already discussed.'

'Patience, *glyká mou*. This is important.' He threaded his fingers through hers, engulfing her hand. Alice wished she didn't enjoy that easy touch so much.

She'd miss it when she went back to England.

'Go on then.'

Deliberately she turned away from his proud, handsome profile, staring over the rough ground where she'd sketched this afternoon. There'd been bright red peacock anemones and carpets of white daisies, delicate pink orchids and so many other flowers she didn't have names for. She could spend days, weeks, years here, painting.

It was paradise.

And not just because of the plants. Or the sunlight or the friendly locals.

Paradise because you've never been happier than here, with Adoni.

She stilled, arrested by what that told her.

'I've thought about how we can achieve that and ensure our son isn't continually in transit between us, especially when he begins school. Continuity will be important.'

Alice sat straighter. What was he leading up to? Continuity? Did that mean their child living with Adoni since he could provide everything money could buy? Alice's tension notched up. Would she have to fight for her rights?

His expression was intent, still as a predator about to strike, or a tycoon about to deliver a *coup de grâce* to some underperforming executive.

Had she misjudged him? Was he going to fight for sole custody? Surely not! That didn't fit with the man she'd come to know and—

'I believe we should raise him together.'

'Sorry, I thought you said—'

'I did. I believe the pair of us should raise him.'

She angled her head as if that might help her read his thoughts but he looked more guarded than ever.

'Define *together*.'

'As a couple. As a mother and father, raising their child in the usual way.'

Alice blinked but Adoni looked just the same. 'You mean *living together*?' Her voice betrayed her, growing hoarse.

'*Ne.* Yes.' He caressed the pad at the base of her thumb. Was it an unconscious gesture or was he trying to soothe her, knowing he'd dropped a bombshell?

'Adoni.' She sat forward, her gaze locked on his. 'You need to spell this out. It sounds like you're talking about us living as…as…'

'Partners. Parents. Lovers.' Each word, in that deep voice, was like a mighty stone dropping into a still pool. Alice felt the ripples grow and crest in waves of emotion.

'You want us to *marry*?' Her voice cracked. Adoni hadn't struck her as conservative but he was Greek and she guessed traditions like marriage and legitimacy might be more important to him than to many.

She had her answer in his instantaneous withdrawal and the blaze of horror in his widening eyes. He slammed against the back of his chair and his hand dropped hers as if he'd discovered it was a live bomb.

'Not that!' He shook his head for good measure. Then, as if reading something in her gaping expression, he continued. 'I don't intend to marry, ever. I'm sure you understand, given my history.'

Alice inclined her head. He meant his mother, who'd married only for money and security. The woman who'd lied and connived and never divulged the identity of Adoni's real father.

Adoni's distaste for marriage was understandable. Yet that didn't diminish her hurt at his horror. Or her poignant sense of loss that it could never be an option.

What was she thinking?

Her nape prickled as she identified the direction of her thoughts.

Was she really pining because Adoni would never offer to marry her? It wasn't as if they loved each other. Marriage would be a farce, a sop to convention because of the child they shared.

Alice clasped her hands tight in her lap, as if by reining in her physical response she might control her wayward thoughts.

'So,' she said slowly. 'You want us to live as a couple.' She paused, watching him nod. 'To be lovers and parents together.'

'A family. Yes.' He leaned towards her then, his mouth curving invitingly.

It's safe for him to get close now he's made it clear you can never be his wife.

Alice cursed the cynical voice in her head and tried to focus. Just because *she* believed in love and marriage didn't mean everyone did.

'But we don't…' She hesitated to use the word *love*. 'You're talking about a permanent commitment?'

His eyebrows lifted as if in surprise. 'Won't raising our son be a permanent commitment?'

'Of course. But that's different.'

'Why? We agreed stability and strong, loving relationships will be best for our child.'

There it was again. That zap of sensation on the words *our child*.

'That doesn't mean we have to *be* together.' Even if her insides were doing cartwheels at the prospect of being Adoni's long-term lover. Of sharing her days and nights with him while they brought up their son together.

Listen to her. Now she was buying into his crazy idea, even down to the sex of their child!

Adoni's gaze dropped to her mouth, then her breasts, completing a leisurely survey then lifting to her eyes. By that time Alice's breathing was short and sharp and hot needles prickled her flesh. She wanted to be outraged but instead identified her reaction as excitement.

She had it bad, this attraction for Adoni.

'We don't have to be together but I *want* to, Alice.' His voice hit that low, resonant note that did disastrous things to her determination to resist. 'You'll be a wonderful mother. You're warm, generous and attractive. I like your down-to-earth attitude and your honesty.'

Honesty? He'd come so far from the man who'd accused her of sleeping with him for gain.

'Thank you, but—'

'Plus, I want you as I've never wanted any other woman.' The words left her speechless, mutely blinking up at him. 'I think we could make each other very happy, Alice.' He reached for her hand again, raising it to his lips and pressing a kiss there that sent hope, desire and all sorts of impossible emotions shivering through her.

'This is very…unexpected.' Alice couldn't think what to say. Her one conviction was that she mustn't—absolutely must *not*—throw herself at him and say yes. Though the temptation was strong. She needed time to consider.

He might have read her mind. 'You need to think about it.' His sober tone conflicted with his heated, hungry eyes. Those spoke a different language, not of caution and negotiation but of rampant ownership. The fire in his eyes made her whole body tingle.

Alice frowned. Adoni, *possessive*?

'You needn't worry that you'll be disadvantaged in any way,' he said quickly, making her wonder how he'd interpreted her frown. 'My legal team has drawn up an agreement so you'll be looked after.'

'Looked after?' She sounded like a parrot but she had trouble following his logic. She'd thought Adoni would look after her, and vice versa. Surely, if they were partners—

'While I'm alive and even if anything should happen to me, you'll be taken care of.'

'I think you need to explain.'

Adoni nodded. When he spoke his tone was brisk. Yet still she saw a glaze of heat in his scrutiny. 'We sign a contract. I will support you with a generous allowance.' He named a sum so large it made her head spin. 'That will continue even if I predecease you, so long as you are supporting our child and he's thriving under your care. But you'll have no other claim on my estate—it will all go to the boy.'

Alice felt her eyes round. Anger spiked that there was any doubt their child would thrive under her care! Was Adoni going to appoint observers to check that?

Then she recalled how his parents had treated him and, though still angry, managed to swallow her pride. He was trying to ensure their baby was well cared for. She couldn't fault Adoni for that.

'And what would I be agreeing to?' Her voice didn't sound like her own.

Adoni shrugged. 'To live as my partner, help bring up our son. Not take any other lovers.'

Did his gaze sharpen on the words?

'And would you make a similar commitment?' Her chin hiked up.

'*Yes*. I have no intention of undermining the family I want to build for our child.'

Our child. There they were again, those magic words. Only this time, instead of making Alice feel warm and fuzzy, they made a warning bell clang discordantly. No matter how tempting it was to think of being Adoni's lover, his partner, this was about the baby. Not them.

Alice shook her head. 'I don't know. It's too...'

'Too what?' Adoni leaned in, his wide shoulders and intent expression crowding her back in the seat.

Too bizarre! A binding contract to ensure she cared for her child and didn't cheat on her lover!

Whoever heard of such a thing?

Adoni, obviously. It was a reminder that, however relaxed she felt with him, they were from different worlds.

'Unexpected,' she said flatly. A weight pushed down on her, crushing her earlier pleasure at being with him.

Clearly that wasn't enough for Adoni. His mouth thinned. She could almost hear his mind working.

'It's more than fair, Alice.' His eyes flashed and his jaw angled up in that unconsciously arrogant expression that both thrilled and annoyed her. 'I've even stipulated that all decisions about the child's future will be mutually agreed between us. I'm trying to make things easier.'

Part of her recognised he was right. In his own outlandish way, he was ensuring their child had a family who loved and cared for it.

'What if I want to do something in addition to being a mother? Like go to art school and work as an artist?' She'd already buried that idea, at least for the foreseeable future, because it would take all her time and resources to care for her baby. But she wanted, one day, to pursue the dream she'd deferred so long.

'Alice.' Adoni took her hand in both of his, his clasp ridiculously reassuring. 'I'm not a bully. Of course you need your art. You're talented and it's a tragedy you haven't had a chance to pursue that properly.' His words buried themselves deep within her. Pleasure glowed at his belief in her.

'I don't intend to give up my business but I'm sure I can delegate more so I spend time with you and our boy. If you want to work too, you should. So long as there's a balance between career and home.'

Alice shook her head, striving to take it all in.

'What?' Adoni's hold tightened. 'What have I said that you don't like?'

She smiled ruefully. 'Nothing. You're being so…reasonable, it's a shock. I thought you might demand I devote myself solely to hearth and home.'

His lips quirked up. 'It's true we Greeks can be traditional about that.' His thumb rubbed the underside of her wrist and her pulse fluttered. 'But I want what's best for our child. I believe that means mutual respect and parents who are happy and fulfilled, not sniping over petty grievances.'

'You don't envisage disagreements?'

'I'm counting on them.' He leaned so close his breath tickled her face and Alice felt heat sear her throat and cheeks. 'I love your spirit. The way you stand up for yourself. I anticipate our love life will be fiery and incredibly satisfying.'

The bloom of damp heat in the space between her legs told Alice she'd enjoy it too.

But beneath it all, like a sour note she couldn't eradicate, was regret. More than regret. Disappointment.

That Adoni would love their baby but never her. He'd excised the very notion and, no matter how tempting it was to believe she could change him with time, she had to face facts. Adoni didn't believe in romantic love. It wasn't even on his radar.

They could have a mutually enjoyable, respectful relationship, dedicated to the well-being of their child.

But there would be no love.

Could she live with that? Give up what, she realised now, she'd hoped to find one day. Could she accept something that was its mere shadow?

She swallowed, tasting that sourness on her tongue.

'You'll have to give me time to think.'

Adoni ended the conference call and shoved his chair from his desk. Here in the tower above the house, he had spectacular three-hundred-and-sixty-degree views. Usually the panorama of sea and land was soothing.

Not today. Not even his company's impending software

release, which promised to be its most successful yet, made him smile.

He stalked to the window facing the coast.

His software enterprise was steadily increasing market share. His plan to widen his investment base with a portfolio of luxury boutique hotels was proving profitable, despite economic uncertainties. Even the Devon property was available for purchase at the price he wanted.

Yet he felt no buzz of satisfaction.

Shoving his hands in his pockets, he surveyed the slope to the beach. Alice had taken that route. She'd talked of capturing some shots of wildflowers for the portfolio she was preparing. No doubt she was immersed in her art.

Her talent made his own capacity with numbers and technology seem a paltry thing, mere money-making.

Because somewhere along the line his passion had become business?

No, he wasn't such a naïve purist. He revelled in his work, got satisfaction out of developing better and more user-friendly software. It had taken talent as well as incredible hard work to achieve what he had.

Yet still he felt that niggle of dissatisfaction.

Adoni peered at the coastal track. Was she coming back yet?

It had been weeks since he'd suggested they live together permanently, yet Alice still hadn't agreed. He'd pulled back, giving her time to consider. Lately, when he'd raised the subject, she'd looked so troubled he hadn't persisted, telling himself to be patient. He'd bided his time. Surely these halcyon days were a precursor to the future he envisaged.

Alice was as responsive as ever. His sex life had never been so good. And living with her had convinced him a long-term arrangement made eminent sense. He felt energised by her presence. Even chatting over dinner was a delight rather than the chore it had sometimes been on dates.

It was only a matter of time before she said yes and signed the agreement that would bind them into a family.

He frowned, his mind snagging on her expression as he'd shown her the contract. Was it the penalty clause for disloyalty that made her hesitate? If she slept with someone else she'd lose all financial support.

But that was non-negotiable. Adoni couldn't countenance the thought of Alice having sex with someone else. His fingers bit into the windowsill.

She was *his*. They'd be a family. He wasn't sharing her with anyone but their child.

As ever, thought of that fragile new life sent a shaft of pleasure/pain through his chest. Pride and excitement vied with fear of what could happen if Adoni didn't take every precaution to protect his son.

He looked at the westering sun, turning the navy blue sea to shades of apricot and neon pink.

It was late, in more ways than one.

He'd been patient long enough.

CHAPTER FOURTEEN

ADONI WAS WAITING for her when Alice entered the master suite, sketchbook in hand. Her skin was flushed despite the broad-brimmed hat that protected her from the sun.

'We need to talk.' He hadn't meant to blurt it out but his phenomenal patience had frayed.

He needed to close this deal. Now.

Besides, when she swept the hat away, releasing a tumble of auburn-tinted hair that caught the dying light like rubies, when her pert breasts pushed with every quick breath against her shirt, it was talk or take her to bed.

For weeks Adoni had revelled in the sex. It was time he developed control.

'Sure.' She surveyed him with her deep slate-blue gaze then turned to put away her art equipment. 'Is there time for a shower first?'

'No.' If she showered he'd join her. There'd be no talking—no *sensible* talking—for hours. 'It's time to sort this.'

She didn't ask what *this* was. She must have been expecting this discussion.

'Okay. But let's go to the pool. I can soak my feet while we chat.'

Adoni nodded and motioned for her to lead the way. His eyes traced the curves of her hips beneath denim shorts and the way her pale T-shirt clung. Was that a slight thickening of her slim waist? He loved her body just as it was, but he eagerly awaited visible signs of pregnancy. The thought of her cradling his child in her body was still one of the most powerfully erotic things he'd ever known.

'You want to talk about the contract?' she said when they

were settled, he in a lounge chair and she on the flagstones, her bare feet in the pool as she leaned back on her hands.

It struck Adoni that this way he saw her only in profile, not face-on.

'We need to prepare for our child's arrival.' Better to mention that than the fact he, Adoni, was unsettled that they hadn't arrived at an agreement. His nights had been spiked lately by dreams where Alice shoved the contract at him then strode off, carrying their infant son whose outstretched arms and cries tore Adoni from sleep.

He set his jaw. That *wasn't* going to happen.

'You're right.' She paused and her forehead wrinkled as she stared across the pool. 'But you're asking a lot, Adoni.'

He locked his jaw. He'd *been* patient. This was the best way to proceed. They'd all win.

'What will it take to convince you?'

Slowly Alice turned. Her expression was more sombre than he'd seen in weeks. Adoni's belly tightened as premonition drilled through him. Had something happened on her outing? She'd been all smiles when she left.

'Tell me about Vassili Petrakis.'

Adoni reared back, shock smacking him.

'What's he got to do with us?'

Alice shrugged. 'I need to understand you before I commit to living with you.'

Adoni strove for control. If hearing this again helped persuade her, what did it matter?

'We thought he was my father. Then we discovered he wasn't.' Adoni kept the words brief. 'He was furious that my mother had deceived him and he'd raised a cuckoo in the nest.' Adoni's skin crawled. He could still hear the bass rumble of disgust in the old man's voice. 'He kicked me out and I've never seen him since.'

Adoni rubbed his collarbone as if there was a phantom ache from the old fracture. Vassili had been so furious that day. When Adoni hadn't instantly obeyed and left the house, Vassili had tried to shove him out of the door. Adoni, angry and heartsore, but above all stunned at the rejection, had lost his footing and crashed onto the stone doorstep. The old man had shut the door so fast he probably didn't even realise Adoni had been injured.

Slim fingers gripped Adoni's other hand. He turned to find Alice leaning close, sympathy in her eyes.

'It must have been dreadful.' Her brow knotted. 'But don't you want to see him again? He raised you after all. He must have felt so betrayed. Maybe he regrets how he behaved.'

Adoni turned his hand, capturing her delicate wrist, feeling the strong pulse hammer there. Alice was nervous. Why?

'I have no interest in seeing him. He disowned me. Barred me from seeing my brothers.' Though of course they were brothers in name only. 'Because of him I was homeless, penniless and I lost my fiancée too.' Which had been a blessing in disguise, but that didn't pardon Vassili's rejection.

Alice blinked, suddenly breathless. Adoni's words stripped the air from her lungs. He'd been *engaged*?

Finally she found her voice. 'Weren't you young to be engaged?'

'Nineteen.' His voice was grim. 'I thought I knew it all. Just as I thought Vassili couldn't be serious about disowning me.'

'What happened? To your fiancée?'

'Nothing.' Adoni's mouth curved up in a smile that made Alice shiver. It looked *feral*. 'When she realised I had no money or prospects she ditched me.'

Alice watched Adoni's face stiffen into an implacable mask. Clearly he'd never forgiven the woman.

Then it hit her—first his mother, then his fiancée, both teaching him women weren't to be trusted. One such betrayal would warp any man's opinion. But two?

No wonder he demanded she sign a contract. Everything had to be checked and double-checked by lawyers, because simple trust was impossible.

Alice sucked in a frantic breath as her stomach hollowed. It felt as if her insides were collapsing. Or maybe that was her stupid daydreams.

Fervently she wished she could turn back the clock to this morning, when they'd laughed together in Adoni's vast bed. He'd teased her, kissing the couple of freckles on her nose, then proceeded to examine her all over, pretending to find and kiss more freckles in the most unlikely places. They'd been so *happy*, so in tune.

She remembered the heavily lined face of the man she'd met this afternoon. The pain in his eyes that she suspected had nothing to do with his physical problems.

'I saw him today.' Just in time she stopped herself from saying *your father*. 'Vassili.'

'You *what*?' Adoni's grip tightened, making her wince. Instantly he released her. 'Where was this?' He drew himself up, his expression ominous. He looked like a warrior preparing for battle.

'Down near the shore. He saw me drawing.'

Adoni breathed deep. On the exhale he whispered a string of soft, savage words in Greek. 'He knew who you were?'

Of course he did. It was a small community and she'd just learned his house sat on the next headland. She could see it now. Adoni must have built here to thumb his nose at the man who'd raised then rejected him. Alice shivered, recalling what Adoni had said about long-held grudges in this part of the world.

Was that the sort of world she wanted her child to grow up in?

'He knew where I was staying. He asked how you were.' Alice had read the effort it took for the older man to ask. With his chunky stature and square face he looked nothing like Adoni but in one thing they were the same—that look of austere pride. Adoni wore it now like a warning sign.

'You didn't answer him?'

Alice rubbed her hands up her suddenly chilled arms. 'I told him you were well. I told him your business is thriving and...'

'He has no right to hear any of that.' Adoni's voice was harsh, like forged metal.

'I felt sorry for him. He's had a stroke, I think. His face was lopsided and he walked with a stick.' It was obvious he'd made a monumental effort to reach her. A man with his physical limitations didn't just happen along the track where she painted. She'd ended up walking him back to the village, concerned despite his protestations.

Adoni said nothing. Nor did his expression soften.

'I think...' She hesitated. 'I'm sure he'd like to see you, maybe make amends.' The old man's sorrow touched her. 'If he contacted you would you...?'

Alice stopped as Adoni's expression flickered.

'He *has* contacted you, hasn't he?'

Adoni shrugged. 'We have nothing to discuss.'

Alice stared. 'I know he did wrong, Adoni. But he was your father. Don't you want to see him? See your brothers?'

The flicker became a scowl. 'He made it clear they're not my brothers.'

'Adoni!' Alice swung her legs out of the pool and knelt before him, putting her arms around him and squeezing tight. But he held himself rigid. There was no softening. No acceptance of the comfort she offered.

'Isn't it worth *trying*?'

Adoni captured her wrists and unwound her arms, distancing her as he held her hands before him. His eyes were hard as diamonds. 'The past is over. What's important is our child. Our life together. When you sign the contract—'

'I'm not saying you can change the past. Just that it's better not to hold hate in your heart.' And distrust. She wanted to tell Adoni she was fighting for *him*—for them, and their child. For she wasn't sure she could commit to a family where her partner was better at grudges and distrust than loving.

Especially now she knew it was love she wanted from this man. She'd finally worked out what all her feelings for him meant. Trust, desire, frustration, pride, tenderness and hope—so much hope.

Together they added up to love.

She'd been falling in love with Adoni from the night she'd barged into him and looked up into those amazing blue-green eyes that shimmered with amusement and tenderness. She'd fallen further the more she knew him. These last weeks, living and laughing with him, had simply set the seal on her emotions.

She was in love with Adoni Petrakis.

She wanted him with all her heart and soul.

But she wasn't prepared to settle for less than love. She needed more.

Even the *hope* of love in the future would do to begin with.

But was he capable of that? Could he weather the inevitable ups and downs of a close personal relationship with positivity and a willingness to meet her halfway?

'You ask too much.'

Maybe she did. Maybe this was crazy, none of her business. But it felt vital she try.

'I know I'm asking a lot.' Alice pressed close, willing him to understand. 'I don't ask you to forgive and forget.

But just listen, that's all. He said his sons —' just in time she stopped herself from saying *your brothers* '—miss you. They want to contact you but feel it would be disloyal while there's a breach between you and Vassili.'

Surely Adoni would relent if it meant reuniting with the young men with whom he'd shared his youth?

'You're not listening, Alice. The past is the past. I want to move on.'

Alice sat back on her heels, drawing her hands from his. Despite the warm air and the heat of the flagstones, a chill enveloped her.

It was tempting to say nothing, to sign his precious contract and hope for the best. But everything inside her screamed that was wrong. It wasn't the way things were supposed to be between two people who truly cared—

'Alice? This has nothing to do with *us*.'

'How can you say that? The past isn't over for you, Adoni. It's driving the present and it's shadowing your future, *my* future. Our *child's* future.'

She hefted a sustaining breath. 'It's not just about you and Vassili. It's deeper than that. You're asking me to sign my life away in a legal contract.' Before he could speak she raised her palm. 'I understand you're wealthy and need to protect that wealth. But—' Alice shook her head '—I want us to be about more than that.'

'What are you saying? That you'll agree to my plan only if I talk to that man?' Adoni looked strained, the flesh tight across the strong bones of his face. 'Or that you're offended by me wanting to protect us all with a written contract? You want to live with me but not accept my terms?'

Alice tried to read his expression. Was that anger there? Scorn? She couldn't tell. Something about the hollow timbre of his voice spoke of disappointment, but maybe she projected her own feelings.

She shook her head. 'I don't know. I'm sorry, I honestly don't know.'

She lifted her knees and wrapped her arms tight round her legs, trying to protect herself from the onslaught of fierce emotions that charged the atmosphere. Her nape prickled as if from static electricity and she wouldn't have been surprised to hear the hiss and crackle of something combusting.

'I *care* for you, Adoni.' She wasn't brave enough to tell him the truth, that she loved him.

'But…?' One of those sleek winged eyebrows that she found so appealing flicked high, making his expression simultaneously superior and disappointed.

'I've been thinking about your contract. I was going to tell you I'm ready to sign—'

Instantly his demeanour changed. Adoni leaned forward, his knuckles gently brushing her cheek. His smile made him a different man. The man she loved. 'That's wonderful!'

Alice pulled back, torn between loss and relief when his hand dropped away.

'But then I thought about what would happen if I got pregnant a second time.' His smile was back, that familiar, slow, delicious one she saw most often in bed. 'It's quite likely, you know. We used a condom last time but I still fell pregnant and you're so—'

'Virile? Insatiable?' He shrugged. 'It's not just me, *glyká mou*. You're as highly sexed as I am.'

Alice flattened her mouth, biting back a retort that it wasn't about being highly sexed. It was about being with the person you *loved*.

'If we are blessed with a second child, or a third, I won't complain.'

She believed him. In fact, Adoni positively beamed. But he hadn't thought this through as she had.

'But what will be your *first* response? You want me to agree in front of lawyers, to lose financial support from you and actually pay a fine if ever I'm caught having an affair. You've arranged it so that if you die and I'm left raising our son...' She blinked, her eyes prickling. Damn it, again she was buying into his belief it was a boy. 'Raising our *child*, someone will check I'm doing a good job before letting me have that allowance.'

'You—'

'Let me finish, Adoni. Please.'

Eyes narrowed, he nodded.

'What that tells me is that you don't trust me. Even now you know me better, you don't *trust* me. You reserve the right to believe I might live down to your worst expectations.'

Alice snatched another shallow breath, her lungs too tight to allow anything more substantial. 'So if I come to you and tell you I'm expecting another baby, will you arrange another paternity test, just to be sure? Will you calculate your travel over the previous months and check where I'd been without you? Perhaps get investigators to see if I've had any male visitors? When will we celebrate—when I break the news or when we get the results back from the lab?'

Adoni's face was stony, the frantic pulse at his jaw the only sign of life.

'And if there's a third pregnancy, do we do it all over again because though you might *want* to trust me, you can't quite manage it? Just as you find it hard to forgive?'

Alice blinked, swallowing tears that threatened, for she knew, she could see in his eyes, that he *wanted* to trust her.

'I know your mother and father hurt you. I know your fiancée let you down. If I could get my hands on that woman I'd make her sorry for how she damaged you. I'm so jealous of her. Because you *loved* her.' Alice gulped, knowing she'd revealed too much. 'I'm sure you didn't make *her* sign on the dotted line and—'

'Which is exactly why a contract is necessary. I've learned my lesson.'

'Not everyone is out to betray you, Adoni. *I'm* not.'

'Yet you find it impossible to prove that by simply signing your name.'

Alice's shoulders slumped. She couldn't get through to him, didn't have the words to make him understand how she felt. She couldn't bear this any more. It felt as if her heart cracked from top to bottom.

'You don't know how much I want to sign,' she whispered. 'If I did I'd have it all, wouldn't I? You and our baby and our life together.'

It was a struggle to swallow over the lump in her throat.

'But every time I've tried I just can't. It doesn't feel *right*, selling myself like a commodity in a deal picked over by lawyers. I don't expect you to love me—I know you don't. But I need *something*. A sign that maybe, one day, you'll smash through that shell you've built around your heart and really care.' She turned and looked away, her gaze turning to the mansion on the next headland.

'I thought if you agreed to listen to Vassili, or meet your brothers, it would be proof your heart hadn't completely hardened—'

'Alice. Don't.' A large hand brushed her cheek, smearing the trickle of moisture she hadn't even noticed. 'Don't cry.' His voice was rough.

Savagely she rubbed her face, banishing the tears, though they tasted bitter at the back of her throat. She got to her feet, her knees as creaky as those of a woman four times her age.

'I'm sorry, Adoni.' She met his eyes, saw a bleakness there that matched what she felt. 'It's totally unreasonable to expect you *not* to insist on a contract. I don't know exactly *what* I want.'

Liar—you want him to love you!

'I just know it's not this.'

Alice drew a shaky breath, waiting for him to argue, to insist. But he said nothing. He looked as shell-shocked as she felt.

Gathering up her strength, she said what she should have weeks ago. 'Thank you for the generous...proposition. It's very tempting but it won't work. When I commit to a man for life I want it to be for love, not convenience.' She swung away, her vision blurring.

'I'd appreciate it if you could arrange my flight back to England. Have your lawyers draw up papers for shared custody, time with you and time with me. I won't fight you on that.'

She swallowed, her face crumpling like her heart as she walked away. 'Goodbye, Adoni.'

CHAPTER FIFTEEN

ADONI SHRUGGED AND straightened his jacket. Tailor-made, it fitted perfectly, but this evening it didn't seem to.

He hooked a finger into his collar, trying to ease the constriction there, though he knew it was just nerves. Even the phantom pain in his collarbone was back.

Too much rode on tonight's outcome.

Everything rode on it.

He'd realised the moment Alice had left him in Greece, even *before* she'd left, that the arrangement she suggested was untenable. He had no intention of sharing their child, like a boomerang flying backwards and forwards between them. Of not seeing Alice except at each handover.

He rubbed the heel of his hand over his clavicle. He knew what he wanted. And he was a man who got what he wanted. Yet that knowledge inspired none of his usual confidence.

For the first time in years Adoni felt nervous. Scared his plan might not work.

Catching the direction of his thoughts, he stiffened his spine and strode to the door of the plush London gallery. He'd never been a coward. He couldn't afford to start now.

The first room was empty. The exhibition wouldn't open for another hour and the gallery was technically closed. In the distance he heard the clatter of plates from a back room—caterers preparing for tonight's party.

Adoni strode deeper, barely glancing at the portraits on the white walls. When he'd come here to see Felix Christow earlier, these works by Alice's mother had moved him immeasurably. They conveyed such depth of emotion, such understanding, it was impossible not to be entranced. Especially when the subject was someone she loved. The portrait of her husband, captured at his drawing board, with his sleeves rolled up and his hair unkempt, conveyed such warmth and affection Adoni felt as if he'd intruded into an intensely private world.

That was the world Alice had inhabited as a child. A world of love and intimacy, of happiness and trust such as Adoni had never known. No wonder she hadn't been ready to accept his bloodless contract!

Murmuring voices drew him into a vaulted space, the second last room in the exhibition.

There she was.

Adoni's heart slammed his ribs so hard it felt as if it had yanked free. That it might at any moment tumble right out of his body.

It had been just a week since he'd seen her but it seemed a century.

His pulse skipped as he realised she wore the dress he'd given her. She'd left it in his home. The sight of it, alone in the empty wardrobe, had reinforced his isolation, his loneliness, after she'd gone.

He'd wrenched it out but, instead of tossing it away, his hands had gentled on the soft fabric she'd worn against her flesh. The next day he'd had it hand-delivered, with a note asking that she keep the gift as proof of goodwill between them.

His relief when she'd accepted had been matched only by his determination to make Alice accept more than a mere dress.

Now the dark blue gown graced her slim form. The beaded bodice scintillated as she moved and the short skirt flirted around her pale legs. Her dark hair, with its rich hint of auburn, was simply styled up, leaving her creamy neck bare except for that glowing opal necklace.

And Adoni wanted her as he'd never wanted any woman in his life.

That was what drove him across the room, heedless of the fear jamming his throat.

'Ah, Mr Petrakis. How good to see you.' Christow, the gallery owner, was calm and urbane, everything Adoni wasn't at the moment. Adoni stared down into Alice's stunned face, feeling the charge of adrenaline rush his body.

He must have responded to Christow's welcome, even answered, but he had no recollection of it. He was so engulfed by emotion as he drank her in he barely noticed the other man leave.

'He was expecting you.' Alice's voice was uneven. The beads over her breasts trembled and shimmered as she drew an unsteady breath.

'Sorry?' Adoni forced himself to focus on Alice's words.

'Felix expected you.' It was a challenge. Or perhaps an accusation.

Adoni shrugged. He wasn't going to apologise for persuading the gallery owner to arrange this time with her. Christow had been only too eager to assist a collector of Adoni's stature.

'I mentioned I'd like an early viewing.'

Who are you kidding, Petrakis? Pride has no place here. It's already done more harm than good.

'I needed to see you.'

Alice lifted her hand to her opal choker, fingers closing around it like a talisman.

'We've said everything, Adoni. Let's leave it to the lawyers.' Her eyes shimmered, over-bright, and he wanted to reach out and pull her close, assure her everything would be okay. Except the curl of raw terror in his gut was proof everything was far from okay.

'No lawyers.'

'Sorry?' Her grasp on the necklace tightened.

'What's between us…' For the life of him Adoni couldn't prevent his gaze dropping to her flat stomach. 'It's not a matter for lawyers.'

If he'd thought that might convince her to listen, he was doomed to disappointment. Her pale face froze and her beautiful mouth tightened.

'I'm sorry, Adoni.' Her voice sounded stretched tight. 'I can't do this. Not here, not now.' A jerky movement indicated her mother's art on the walls. 'This is already… difficult.'

He stepped closer. 'I can imagine it is. But wonderful too. To see so much of your mother's work in one place must be gratifying.'

Slate-blue eyes caught his, widening as if she were surprised at his understanding.

'Your mother was very talented. Like you.'

Instantly Alice shook her head. 'There's no comparison. I'm just—'

'An incredibly gifted artist.' He could resist no longer. Adoni reached out and touched her bare arm, his fingertips tingling at the contact. She stilled, her breath locking in her lungs just like his. The touch became a caress, light as a windblown leaf, and he felt her shiver.

But she didn't pull away.

His fingers encircled her arm, gently capturing her.

'You're right,' he murmured, inhaling the aroma of sweet blossom and femininity that was Alice's signature scent. 'This isn't the place.'

He pulled gently, inviting her into the exhibition's final room. 'There's something I want you to see. *Please.*'

Adoni's tension eased, just a little, when she moved with him. They turned a corner, into a dimly lit space where lights illuminated the sole painting in the room. An exquisite portrait in oils of a mother and child.

Alice froze. He heard the hiss of her breath.

'How?' She swallowed hard. 'Felix didn't mention this!' She took a step closer, eyes on the painting, and Adoni released his hold.

'It was a late inclusion.' Adoni didn't spare the painting a glance. All his attention was on Alice and the stark emotion in her taut frame. Had he done the right thing? 'I hoped you'd like seeing it again—'

'*You* arranged this?' She swung round and met his stare, her eyes shocked.

Hell! It was meant to be a pleasant surprise.

'I've been negotiating for weeks to buy it. I was going to give it to you—' he paused, not wanting to say the words, but knowing he must '—when you agreed to stay with me.'

Alice blinked and, to his horror, tears glistened in her eyes. Furiously she blinked them back. 'That was a very kind gesture.'

Kind? He wasn't kind. He'd wanted to make her as happy as he'd known he'd be when she agreed to be his.

Except it hadn't worked out that way, had it?

'I'm sorry. I didn't mean to upset you.'

Alice stared up into Adoni's strong face, noting the meticulously shaved jaw, the tautness in those proud features and the flicker of unease in his eyes. She'd never sensed such vulnerability in him. She didn't know what to make of it.

'You didn't upset me. You…surprised me.' She turned to the portrait, her pulse thumping madly. It showed a young woman with auburn hair and laughing blue eyes. On her lap sat a little girl of three, clasping a ragged old teddy. Alice knew she was three because her parents had told the story often, of how they'd had to cajole her to sit still long enough for her mother to complete the self-portrait. Of how Alice had squirmed and shifted until her father handed her Old Ted.

'It was the last painting of hers that my father sold. He

didn't want to part with it.' Her throat closed on the words. Money had been so tight when David offered them somewhere to live.

'It's yours.' Adoni's voice was gravel.

'But I can't.' She swung to face him. 'I didn't accept your—'

'This is a gift. No strings attached. It should never have left your family.' His voice softened. 'It belongs with you, Alice. I know how important family is to you. You need to have this.'

'But…' His expression stopped her protests. She couldn't define what she saw there, except that it was unfamiliar and compelling. Emotion rippled through her, right to that place inside that had felt hollow since the day she'd left Greece, left Adoni.

Abruptly, to her horror, tears filled her eyes again.

'Don't, *karthia mou*.' His warm hand cupped her cheek, his thumb stroking the moisture away, making her shudder with the effort of restraint. She wanted to bury her head against him, wrap him close and not let him go. She'd been so *lonely* without him. As if she'd left part of herself behind in Greece.

'It's too much.' She blinked and lifted her chin.

His eyes captured hers. 'It's yours, Alice, as it should always have been. It's a work of great beauty and passion and I want you and our child to have it.'

Alice's mouth crumpled. It would be so much easier if she could dislike Adoni, but that was impossible. With every word he made her decision harder to bear.

'If it makes you feel better about accepting, perhaps you'd consider doing me a favour in return?'

'What's that?' Alice gave up trying to pretend she wasn't crying. She sniffed, wiping her eyes.

'Be with me when I meet Vassili and his sons.'

Alice's mouth dropped open. 'You're meeting them?'

The grim lines around Adoni's mouth and the tension in his tall frame gave his answer. 'Yes.' He lifted a hand to his collarbone then dropped it. 'I've been thinking about what you said.' He shook his head. 'I've thought of nothing else. And I decided you were right. I've been a coward.'

'Adoni!' She reached out to touch him, then curbed the gesture, withdrawing her hand. 'You're not—'

'I am.' He straightened to his full, impressive height. 'I pretended family didn't matter. That the past didn't matter, but I was living a lie.' His voice softened. 'So I rang him.'

'You did?' Alice didn't hesitate this time. She grasped his hand, feeling the tremor that ran through him. Worry stabbed her. She'd been so ready to give advice, to tell him what was wrong with his life. But who was she to judge? 'Was it...?'

'It was difficult. Stilted.' Adoni's mouth rucked up at one side. It wasn't a smile yet Alice's heart flipped over. 'I'm not sure about forgiving him, but I'm willing to see. And I want to see the boys. I've missed them.' He covered her hand with his. 'Thank you, Alice. Without you giving me a kick I'd never have made the first move.'

'I didn't do anything. I—'

'You did, *karthia mou*.'

The expression in his eyes, that caressing tone of voice did terrible things to her willpower.

'I wish you wouldn't say things I don't understand. You know I—'

'*Karthia mou* means *my heart*.'

Alice's own heart gave a mighty leap at his words.

'*S'agapó*, Alice. I love you.' He lifted her shaking hand to his mouth and kissed it, slow and gentle, and suddenly her knees were so wobbly she thought she'd collapse. Except he lashed his other arm around her, enfolding her in protective heat.

'Adoni? I don't understand. You don't do love. You don't trust or—'

'*Didn't*. Past tense.' He smiled and it was like sunshine after a month of grey skies, warming her to the core. Yet his eyes didn't smile. His eyes were sombre. 'I thought I loved Chryssa but I was too young to realise it was infatuation. What I feel for you is far beyond that. And, before you ask, it's not just because of the baby. It's *you*, the woman you are, the way you make me feel.'

He pressed another kiss to her hand, her palm this time, and desire shot through her like flaming ribbons. Desire, hope and disbelief. This couldn't be happening.

'*Tha doso ta panta gia na ime mazí sou.*'

Before she could ask he translated.

'I will give anything to be with you. Anything.'

'Adoni?' Her voice cracked. It was too much—far too much—after a week nursing a shattered heart. 'What do you want from me?'

'*You*. I want you, Alice. On any terms you like. Come and live with me, or I'll live with you in Devon. Or marry me.' He paused, his features grave. 'Above everything I want to marry you, but I understand that might be asking too much just yet.'

Alice wished she were strong enough not to reveal how his words affected her, but she wasn't. This week had sapped her strength. Walking away from the man you loved did that.

She clung to him, fingers curling around his. 'Don't talk like that! I know you don't want to marry.' It hurt that he'd say it, when she knew it wasn't possible.

For answer he scooped her up in his arms and strode to the padded bench seat in front of the portrait. He sat and settled her on his lap. Alice felt the hammer of his heart against her and his rough breathing teased her hair.

'I want marriage, Alice, because I want you, for ever.

No contracts, no lawyers, just two people pledging themselves. I *trust* you, Alice. I believe in you.'

She stared up into those stunning eyes and realised he spoke the truth.

Something caught at her chest. Hope?

'When you left I knew I'd been wrong, clutching the past. I knew I wanted you, no matter what. I love you and I want us to be together, simply because we love each other.' His voice dropped to a low note that tugged at her very core. 'I want a chance to prove myself and win your love, Alice. However long it takes.'

It was too much to take in. Too much like the daydreams she'd harboured though she'd tried to be sensible. She shook her head. Instantly he stiffened.

'Please, Alice. I need you. Give me a chance.'

'I'm trying to understand.'

'Maybe you'll understand this.' He tilted her chin and placed his mouth on hers. It was a gentle kiss, so tender, so tentative. A mere brush of soft lips, the silken slide of his tongue, the shuddering breath of a man on the edge.

Suddenly it was too much, and not enough. Her caution disintegrated and desperate yearning took over. Alice speared her hands through his thick hair. She opened her mouth, sucking his tongue inside. Adoni met her caress for caress, till she saw stars and her whole body was afire.

When he pulled back enough to meet her eyes, he looked both triumphant and desperate.

'Tell me you'll give me a chance. I need—'

'You don't need a chance, Adoni.' Alice kissed the corner of his mouth, stunned and grateful that she had the right to. 'I fell in love with you in Greece. I think I even began falling for you that first night.'

There was awe in those eyes that ate her up. And pride and possessiveness and love. Alice guessed they mirrored what was in hers.

Happiness welled, a surge of glorious feeling such as she'd never known. Here, on Adoni's lap, surrounded by those strong arms, caught in his hard embrace, Alice felt she'd finally come home.

'You're willing to take a chance on me, Alice?'

'I am, Adoni. If you are.'

'Always, *karthia mou*. For ever.'

EPILOGUE

'READY, *KARTHIA MOU*?'

Alice looked up into dancing eyes. Eyes as bright as the sea, as bright as the joy she'd found with this man. A little shimmy of excitement wriggled through her. Every day with Adoni was an adventure in love.

'Of course. So long as you promise not to drop me.'

Those wicked eyebrows rose, giving her darling husband a devilish look that always made her pulse race. 'It would take more than a couple of steps to make me let you go, Alice.'

He drew her close to his hard chest, reminding her how very strong he was, and how easily he'd scooped her off her feet. Her thrumming pulse quickened. She loved his strength and protectiveness even if occasionally she had to battle his desire to wrap her and Sophia in cotton wool.

Alice glanced down at the pram parked just inside the open door to the home Adoni had built for them. Sophia Rose Petrakis was fast asleep. With her rosebud mouth and eyes the colour of the sea, she was more beautiful than Alice could have imagined. And she was the light of their lives. Adoni had fallen for their daughter in an instant, despite his earlier conviction they were having a boy. Seeing her husband and daughter together was one of life's most precious gifts.

'She'll be fine for a few moments.' Adoni's deep voice soothed. 'Long enough for me to carry my bride over the threshold.'

'Bride? We've been married a year!' But Alice laughed as he strode into the vestibule and slowly lowered her to the floor.

'But this is the first home we've made together. We needed to mark the occasion.' His meaning was clear.

'You have sex on the brain, Mr Petrakis.'

A slow tilt of his mouth and Alice was swaying against him, wrapping her arms around him.

'And that's bad?' he purred, cupping her face, his hands gently caressing her cheeks.

Emotion welled. She was so very lucky. Who'd have thought life would be so good?

'Alice? Is something wrong?'

Instantly she shook her head then pressed her mouth to his. His kiss reminded her of everything that was right in their lives. Love and trust and a determination to work at a relationship that would last a lifetime.

They spent their time between London and Greece. Adoni had even offered to make a home on the estate where she'd once lived. But the beautiful period property had been David's home, his dream, not hers. So Adoni had found this site looking over the coast nearby, and built a home for them here. A home that would echo with children's laughter and give space for her painting and allow Adoni to work whenever they decided to live in England.

'No, *agape mou*.' The Greek words came easily to her now. 'There's nothing at all wrong. You make me so happy I sometimes can't quite believe how lucky I am.'

'Not lucky, Alice. Loved.' He dipped his head to hers and kissed her with such joy and tenderness that her heart sang.

* * * * *

MILLS & BOON

Coming next month

IMPRISONED BY THE
GREEK'S RING
Caitlin Crews

Atlas was a primitive man, when all was said and done. And whatever else happened in this dirty game, Lexi was his.

Entirely his, to do with as he wished.

He kissed her and he kissed her. He indulged himself. He toyed with her. He tasted her. He was unapologetic and thorough at once.

And with every taste, every indulgence, Atlas felt.

He felt.

He, who hadn't felt a damned thing in years. He, who had walled himself off to survive. He had become stone. Fury in human form.

But Lexi tasted like hope.

"This doesn't feel like revenge," she whispered in his ear, and she sounded drugged.

"I'm delighted you think so," he replied.

And then he set his mouth to hers again, because it was easier. Or better. Or simply because he had to, or die wanting her.

Lexi thrashed beneath him, and he wasn't sure why until he tilted back his head to get a better look at her face. And the answer slammed through him like some kind of cannon-ball, shot straight into him.

Need. She was wild with need.

And he couldn't seem to get enough of it. Of her.

The part of him that trusted no one, and her least of all, didn't trust this reaction either.

But the rest of him—especially the hardest part of him—didn't care.

Because she tasted like magic and he had given up on magic long, long time ago.

Because her hands tangled in his hair and tugged his face to hers, and he didn't have it in him to question that.

All Atlas knew was that he wanted more. Needed more.

As if, after surviving things that no man should be forced to bear, it would be little Lexi Haring who took him out. It would be this one shockingly pretty woman who would be the end of him. And not because she'd plotted against him, as he believed some if not all of her family had done, but because of this. Her surrender.

The endless, wondrous glory of her surrender.

Continue reading
IMPRISONED BY THE
GREEK'S RING
Caitlin Crews

Available next month
www.millsandboon.co.uk